COLDER THAN ICE

David Patneaude

Albert Whitman & Company
Morton Grove, Illinois

Patneaude, David.
Colder than ice / David Patneaude.
p. cm.
Summary: Josh Showalter, an insecure and overweight sixth-grader,
hopes for a new start when he transfers to a school in northern
Idaho, but he and his new friends are soon the target of a
cold-hearted bully.
ISBN 0-8075-8135-6 (hardcover)
[1. Interpersonal relations—Fiction. 2. Schools—Fiction.
3. Overweight—Fiction. 4. Bullies—Fiction. 5. Asperger
syndrome—Fiction. 6. Idaho—Fiction.] I. Title.
PZ7.P2734Co 2003 [Fic]—dc21 2003002095

Design by Mary-Ann Lupa.

*For more information about Albert Whitman & Company,
visit our web site at www.albertwhitman.com.*

To Jasper and Kai, future readers.

And thanks to Brenda, Kathryn, Kirby, and Sylvie, for playing a "critical" role in the shaping of this story.

❄ Contents ❄

1 A Fresh Start 7

2 The Natural 17

3 Student Council President 32

4 Christmas Is Coming 38

5 Canaries 45

6 Weight 56

7 Just Another Kid 67

8 Poor Rooney's Pond 74

9 Out of Control 80

10 The FBI Arrives 91

11 Surprise Package 97

12 Hitting the Ice 107

13 Deep Trouble 126

14 Superheroes 135

15 Threats 141

16 Evidence 150

17 Cruising 157

❄ 1 ❄

A Fresh Start

J oshua Snowater?" The secretary looked up from her desk. Her voice was gravelly and loud. She peered at the two kids waiting in the office: Josh and the small boy sitting next to him.

"Showalter," Josh said.

She held the piece of paper at arm's length. "Showalter," she said. "So it is." She pulled a tissue from a box and blew her nose. Trumpet sounds bounced off the walls. The small boy jumped. "Allergies," she said. She wadded up the tissue and shot it toward a wastebasket fifteen feet away. It popped in perfectly, and she raised her fists in triumph. "Eat your heart out, Shaq!" she boomed.

The small boy edged closer to Josh.

"Your teacher, Ms. Murphy, just called," the secretary told Josh. "She'll be sending a student to take you to your classroom in a couple minutes."

"Okay." He played back his dad's words from the night before—*a chance for a fresh start*. He wanted that chance. He wondered if he could be somebody besides one of the pack—okay student, okay athlete, kind of overweight but okay looking. What would it be like to be *somebody*?

But that prospect didn't make him less nervous. He wasn't eager to get to his classroom. He wasn't looking forward to any of this: new town on Idaho's skinny panhandle, new school, new teacher, new kids. And a kindergarten-to-seventh-grade school? What was up with that?

Back in Seattle, sixth grade was the start of middle school. Here he had almost two more years with little kids, then two years of junior high before he'd get to the high school where his dad had just started teaching. By then he'd have whiskers and size-twelve feet and be listening to opera.

The secretary stared. "Why the long face, buddy boy?"

He shrugged.

"It's only giving up your freedom. It's only sitting at a desk six hours a day while the world dances along without you." She smiled. "It's only school." She went back to her papers.

A kid—a skinny third- or fourth-grade boy with bed-head—skidded into the office and hurried up to the secretary's desk. She took her time looking up, and when she did there was a frown on her round face. "Yes, Mr. Speed Demon?"

The kid waved a piece of paper at her. "I'm supposed to give this to Mrs. Drager."

"*I'll* do that," the secretary said. "Mrs. Drager is busy."

"My teacher—Mrs. Stanwood—said me, *I'm* supposed to."

The secretary snatched the paper from the kid's hand. "Our former principal taught me a lasting lesson, young man—*my* job was to keep folks away from his door so he could do *his* job. I'm sure Mrs. Drager feels the same way."

The kid's mouth hung open, but he didn't say anything.

"Now go back to your classroom."

The boy shuffled away. Josh felt sorry for him, and sorrier for himself. So far, not so good. So far, this school seemed like a step backward. Mrs. Nordlund, the secretary at his old school, had been a peach. This secretary was more like a prune. But at least it was a short week. The Thanksgiving holiday was coming, and on Thursday he'd have one thing for sure to be thankful for: surviving his first three days. He turned to the kid next to him. "What grade are you in?"

"Fuwst."

"First?"

The kid nodded.

"Your first day, too?"

The kid shook his head. "I have to go to speech ferapy today."

A moment later a gray-haired woman peeked through the door. "Ready, Anthony?"

The little guy bounced up and walked out with his rescuer.

Josh stood and looked at the nameplate on the secretary's desk: Mrs. Benedict. Beyond her, behind a mostly closed door, a woman—the principal, he guessed—was talking on the phone. The name on the door was Mrs. Drager.

Mrs. Benedict eyed him. He sat back down—too quickly. The chair was small—a little kid's chair—and it creaked under his weight. Sensing disaster, he jerked his bottom into the air and waited. The chair stood fast. He eased himself down again, shifting his attention to his ankles, where the legs of his jeans were bunched at the tops of his shoes. They reminded him of the stack of pancakes he'd downed for breakfast.

He'd told his mom no more "huskies," which meant she had to get two sizes bigger—size 18—to fit him in the waist. "Look at the cuffs," she'd said. "They'll be shredded in a week." But he was old enough to have some say: "This is how all the kids wear jeans; they're perfect," he'd told her. Now he wasn't so sure.

He looked around at the walls—pictures of mountains and lakes and famous people reading books; posters with rules for dealing with bullies; a sign that said MOUNTAIN VIEW SCHOOL, HOME OF THE HIGHCLIMBERS, above a case filled with trophies and ribbons and plaques and newspaper articles.

He got up carefully and walked to the case. Some of the awards were for sports, some were for classroom stuff—spelling bees, math competitions. One newspaper article, yellowed with age, was about a girl who had placed second at the state spelling bee. A new one reported on a boy—Corey Kitchens, age thirteen, student council president at Mountain View—who had won a countywide free-throw contest and was moving on to the state competition. Josh studied the photo of the kid: Free-throw Championship T-shirt, ball tucked under his arm, trophy held high, cocky smile on his face.

Josh pictured himself in the photo: ball, trophy, T-shirt (just a little tight), regular smile on a round face. He could shoot free-throws, maybe better than Corey Kitchens. After all, Josh had practically grown up in gyms. Maybe someday he'd be the free-throw champ. Maybe he'd get chosen for student council. Maybe he'd even have a thin face and clothes that fit.

A clock near the door read 9:20. His mom would be at her new job in Coeur d'Alene, his dad would be at the high school. His sister, Lindsay? Preschool, where she'd probably made a dozen friends by now. It was harder in sixth grade, when everybody already had their friends, old and new. He thought about his old friends—Charles, Ahmed, Little Joe. What were they up to? They said they would miss him, but did they? They had each other; right now he had no one, and no prospects.

Yeah, he could wait for that student to come and get him. Even with only Mrs. Benedict for company.

He heard voices in the hall. A tall woman

in a long green coat walked into the office, followed by a kid about Josh's age. His hair was the brownish color of Josh's, but the resemblance ended there. His skin had the fragile, almost-white, almost-shiny look of eggshells, and he was thin and small. He glanced toward Josh, but not really at him, more like over his shoulder. Josh found himself staring at the kid's eyes—the brightest, bluest blue he'd ever seen, as if they had lights behind them.

The woman went up to the counter and waited for Mrs. Benedict to look up. She didn't. "My son is beginning school here today," the woman said finally.

Mrs. Benedict squinted at the woman and kid. "Name?"

"His name is Silverthorn. Mark Silverthorn."

Mrs. Benedict smiled. "Now *that's* what I call a *name*." She leafed through some papers.

"*Next* Monday," Mrs. Benedict said. "Not due until *next* Monday."

"We were able to arrive earlier. Is that acceptable?"

"The earlier the better!" Mrs. Benedict roared. "The early bird gets the chocolate!" She wrote something on a piece of paper.

"Good," the woman said. "Will you take

him to his teacher?"

"Oh, I don't do *that*. *I'm* needed *here*. I'm kind of like the moat, and Mrs. Drager's office is the castle. There's a student coming to get Mr. Snowater, though." She nodded in Josh's direction. "They'll be in the same classroom."

The woman turned to look at Josh for the first time. Her skin, her eyes, were the same as Mark's—eggshell pale, glacier blue. "Wonderful," she said, smiling. "Perhaps you two can get acquainted." She gave her son a quick hug and a long look. "I'll see you at home this afternoon, Mark," she said, and walked out the door.

Mark turned toward Josh, but his eyes still avoided Josh's face. They focused their blueness on the wall behind him, and for an instant Josh had to look to see what was so interesting. Nothing but plain old paint. "MR. SNOWATER?" Mark said. His voice was high-pitched thunder—louder than Mrs. Benedict's, even—rolling around the room, getting under Josh's skin.

Josh forced himself to stand. He shook his head. "My name's Josh *Showalter*." He took a step forward and stuck out his hand, but Mark flung up his hands shoulder-high, like little shields. He threw back his head and laughed uproariously, as if Josh had just poked him with a long stick in his most ticklish place.

Josh dropped his hand. What was up with this guy?

Another boy trudged into the office. He was nearly as big as Josh, nearly as wide. His face was round and freckled and topped with reddish-blond hair. His jeans bunched at the ankles, too. He gnawed nervously at his fingers.

"I'm here for the new kid," he said to Mrs. Benedict through his knuckles. But before she could say anything, he spotted Josh. He stopped gnawing. His face froze, then broke into a broad smile. "*You're* the new kid?"

"One of 'em. Mark's new, too."

The kid ignored Mark. He just looked Josh up and down. "You're big," he said. "You're *big*."

Josh nodded. Where did this guy leave his manners?

"You're in sixth grade?"

"Uh-huh," Josh said. "So's Mark."

"What do you weigh?"

"Same as you, probably."

"I think you're heavier. Twenty pounds, maybe."

"So?" What was this guy's problem? Was there anybody normal in this school?

"Nothin'." The smile faded. "Just curious."

Mrs. Benedict held up some papers. She

looked at the newest, weirdest arrival. "Both of these gentlemen, Mark Silverthorn and Joshua *Showalter*, are to go with you, Alex. Give these forms to Ms. Murphy as soon as you get to your classroom."

Alex took the papers. "Okay. Can do. Right away, Mrs. Benedict." He'd lost his trudge; he hurried across the office. "Let's go, guys."

Josh grabbed his backpack and followed them out the door. "Long faces are for horses, buddy boy," Mrs. Benedict called after him.

✳**2**✳
The Natural

*T*wo of you?" Ms. Murphy, young and dark-haired, met them at the classroom door, wearing a smile. Friendly, Josh thought with relief. Normal, maybe. "Where did you find *two*, Alex?"

Alex handed her the papers.

"Good," she said, shuffling them through her fingers, glancing. "Now who's Mark and who's Joshua?"

"I AM MARK." Mark's voice bounced around the classroom, reminding Josh of the booming voice of a guy who peddled fish at the Pike Place Market in Seattle.

Ms. Murphy blinked. "We're glad you could join us early, Mark."

"I am, also," Mark said, gazing over her shoulder. Ms. Murphy reached out her hand to shake, but Mark's hands flew up again. His head tipped back. He laughed raucously. Ms. Murphy's arm hung in the air. The classroom went silent. Mark stopped laughing and stared out the window, as if wishing he were somewhere else.

"And you're Joshua?" Ms. Murphy bravely held her hand out to him, and he took it. They shook. He looked her in the eye, the way his dad had taught him. Maybe Mark didn't have a dad.

They'd moved to the front of the classroom. Josh could feel a couple dozen sets of eyes on him. He checked the bottoms of his jeans to see how much they were bunching. He sucked in his stomach. "Josh."

"Nice to have you here, Josh," Ms. Murphy said. "Before you both sit down, would you mind telling the class where you're from, and what brought you to Rathdrum, Idaho?"

Josh didn't like standing up in front of people and talking. But he figured he had no choice. "Seattle," he blurted out. He couldn't remember what he was supposed to say next.

He looked around the room for a friendly face. In the back corner sat a blond girl with glasses. She smiled at him, amused but friendly.

"And what brought you here, Josh?"

Josh kept his eyes on the girl. She smiled again. "My dad's a teacher. He got a job teaching and coaching basketball and track at Lakeland High School. He's been here since school started. The rest of the family had to stay in Seattle until our house sold. Now my mom's an accountant in Coeur d'Alene."

"Any brothers or sisters?"

"A sister. Lindsay. She's four."

"Good. We hope you're happy here." She turned to Mark, who was staring out the windows. "Mark?"

"Is it snowing?" he said. Every face in the room shifted hopefully toward the windows. Josh squinted his eyes, but he couldn't see even a flake of snow.

Ms. Murphy looked out at the sky. "The weatherman says later in the day is a possibility. Nothing now, Mark."

"I don't like snow," he said, and a murmur moved across the classroom like a wave. Looks passed between kids like secret notes: What kid doesn't like snow?

"Where do we sit?" Mark asked.

"Can you tell us where you're from, first?" Ms. Murphy said.

"Minnesota," Mark said.

"And what brought you here?"

"My father's job." So Mark *did* have a dad.

"And what does he do?"

Mark hesitated. "He helps families."

Ms. Murphy studied him for a moment, as if she was about to ask him what that meant. Then she thought better of it. "Interesting. Brothers or sisters?"

Mark spread his arms wide, his hands open to the class. "I BELIEVE WE ARE ALL BROTHERS AND SISTERS." More looks—smirks this time. Josh edged away from him. Ms. Murphy stared, as if she wanted to peer inside his skull.

She studied one of the papers in her hand. "Oh," she said under her breath. "Oh." She glanced at Mark, who was back to gazing out the window. "Thank you both for sharing," she said finally, attempting a smile. "Class, can we give them a sixth-grade welcome?"

The class cheered and clapped while Ms. Murphy escorted Mark and Josh to their chairs. They were to sit together at a table with the blond-haired girl. The nametag taped to the surface in front of her said "Skye Fisher, Rookie."

"Skye, why don't you show Mark and Josh

where to find supplies so they can make nametags," Ms. Murphy said. "The rest of you can read silently while I take care of some paperwork."

On the way to the supply cabinet, Josh noticed Alex's smile, aimed his way. It felt good to have a stranger glad to see you. He smiled back.

Josh and Mark made nametags: "Mark Silverthorn, Rookie," and "Josh Showalter, Rookie." Skye suggested the "rookie" part because they all were new to Mountain View. She'd started in September.

"We can be the rookie table," she said. Josh wasn't sure he wanted to be known as a rookie; he was trying to fit in, not stick out. But he would go along with it, at least for now.

When they were done, Mark pulled a fancy-looking camera—black with lots of chrome and buttons and glass—from his backpack and began messing around with it. He took pictures of Ms. Murphy, Skye and Josh, and some other kids, who shared whispers and those smirky looks again. When Ms. Murphy's back was turned, they held imaginary cameras to their faces and took imaginary pictures of the scene outside the window. Imaginary snow, Josh figured. He expected Ms. Murphy to say something to Mark, but she acted as if having a classroom photographer was nothing new to her.

After silent reading they had math, then language arts, where Ms. Murphy talked about cinquain poetry. Josh already knew how to do the math; he'd already learned about cinquain poems at his old school. He felt a little better. So far the work wasn't harder here. He wouldn't start out at Mountain View behind everyone else.

The wall clock moved to 11:10. The lunch bell rang.

"You guys play soccer?" Skye asked, getting up from her chair.

"Fullback," Josh said. "My team just finished its season 9 and 1." He didn't say anything about the long minutes he'd spent on the sidelines while the coach let the other guys get most of the playing time.

"Awesome," Skye said. "If we hurry through lunch, we'll have a lot of time for soccer. Recess doesn't end till noon."

"I've seen soccer," Mark said. He slipped his camera into a case, slung it over his shoulder, and stood.

Skye gave him a little frown, then headed for the door. "Let's go."

They wolfed down lunch in a noisy cafeteria

that smelled just like the cafeteria at Josh's old school. Outside, the playground was big and grassy, with bald patches of sandy mud. The far half had soccer goals at each end. Two groups of kids were gathered in the center of the field.

"Come on!" Skye said. "They're already choosing up!"

They jogged to the field. The air was frost going into Josh's lungs, white vapor coming out. Snow weather, maybe.

They angled toward the bigger group. In it were some boys and a few girls Josh remembered from his class, and other kids he didn't recognize. Some looked older. Seventh-graders, probably. He felt the new-kid-at-school lump getting bigger in his throat.

Everyone was just standing around. "What are you guys doing, Hallie?" Skye asked one of the girls.

"Waiting for Corey's little meeting to break up."

"Why do we always have to wait for him?"

Hallie turned up her palms in a who-knows? gesture.

"What are they doing?" Skye asked, but she didn't get an answer. She glared at the smaller cluster of kids: Alex and two older guys. One was tall, with blondish-brown hair. He wore a Stanford sweatshirt with the sleeves cut away to show off broad shoulders and biceps that stood out like knots on a rope. He had a familiar face. It took Josh a moment to figure out why.

He was the kid from the trophy case. Corey What's-his-name. The free-throw champ. The student council president. Mr. Popularity. Mr. Guy-in-charge. What would it be like to be all those things, to have kids standing around waiting for you to tell them how high to jump?

When Alex finished talking, all three of them looked toward the big group. Toward Josh. He was sure of it. Corey laughed, then said something. The mood changed: serious, all of a sudden.

"WHY ARE WE WAITING?" Mark said.

Corey swaggered toward them, trailing the other two like lint balls. "Me and Bunk are captains," he announced.

"Again?" Skye said.

"You don't like it, *Skye*?"

"It's not fair, *Corey*."

"Then don't play."

Skye's cheeks flushed pink; she stuck out her jaw. "I'm playing."

Corey looked at Josh, then Mark. "Why don't you tell us who your new friends are," he said to Skye.

"They can tell you themselves, if they want."

"Why wouldn't they?" He eyed Mark up and down. "You want to tell me who you are, right, kid?"

Mark looked past Corey's wide shoulder, smiling, as if he were on the inside of an in-joke. His eyes sparked.

"What's that stupid smile for?"

"I believe you already have ascertained my name."

"'I believe you already have ascertained my name'? Where'd you learn to talk?"

Mark smiled wider.

"You know what? I *heard* your name but I don't quite *believe* it. *Silverthorn*? What kind of name is *Silverthorn*? And why don't you look at me when I'm talking?"

Mark looked at the ground. "A family name."

"Where you from?"

"Minnesota."

"You don't *sound* like you're from Minnesota," Corey said. "You don't *look* like you're from Minnesota. I would've guessed,

25

like, *Mars*." He laughed a phony laugh and eye-balled his buddies. Bunk forced a chuckle; Alex joined in with a weak giggle.

"Mars no longer supports life," Mark told the dirt at his feet.

"*'Mars no longer supports life,'*" Corey parroted. He narrowed his eyes at Mark, who didn't notice. "What a loser."

"Let him alone, Corey," Skye said.

Corey shook his head at Skye, laughed his phony laugh again, and shifted his attention to Josh. "The other new kid," he said. The cold look left his eyes; he smiled what looked like a real smile.

"Josh Showalter." Josh didn't want to get on anyone's bad side on his first day, and this guy wasn't just anyone.

"I know," Corey said. "I've heard about you. I've heard your dad's the new coach at Lakeland High."

Josh stood a little taller. "Basketball and track."

"Right. And you're probably good at sports, too."

"Fairly good."

"*'Fairly* good.' I bet you're better than fairly good."

"I don't know," Josh said. This guy was

okay, after all. Skye and Mark had been kind of asking for it.

Corey stuck out his hand. "I'm Corey Kitchens." Josh shook it.

"Time's wasting away, Corey," Bunk said.

"Okay. Let's get to choosing." Corey looked over the group, then let his eyes stop on Josh. "I'll take the Joshster," he said.

Josh couldn't believe it: *the first one chosen!* This never would have happened at his old school. He walked over and stood by Corey, who gave him a high five and another smile. Josh tried not to grin, but he couldn't help it. He looked at Skye and Mark. Neither looked happy for him. Skye's nose was scrunched up, as if she were smelling something bad. Mark frowned at the ground. Maybe they were jealous.

Bunk chose another older kid, then it was Corey's turn again. They picked until each team had eight. Skye was the last choice on Corey's team. Mark, dead last, ended up with Bunk.

Josh moved toward a fullback position.

"Where you goin', Josh?" Corey asked.

"I play fullback," Josh said. "Usually." Suddenly he was afraid Corey was going to send him back to the sidelines.

"Not on this team," Corey said. "I want you

27

up front where you can knock in some goals. You take striker." He raised his voice so everyone could hear him. "We'll let Skye play fullback. We'll keep her behind us where we don't have to look at her." He laughed a donkey-meets-hyena laugh. Bunk and Alex joined in. Josh put on a smile—because he got to play forward, he told himself—but he couldn't look at Skye as she walked back toward the goal for the kickoff.

Josh soon discovered he wasn't the fastest kid on the field—that would be Corey or Skye—but he did a good job of playing his position. And every time he was open, Corey, a midfielder, would try to get him the ball. Halfway through recess, Josh snuck behind Mark, Corey gave him a perfect pass, and he punched the ball past the goalie. He'd scored!

"A natural," Corey said as the team—most of them, anyway—high-fived at midfield. Skye hung back at her spot.

Bunk yelled at Mark. "You stink, kid!" But Mark didn't even look up. He was studying some red and yellow leaves that had swirled into a small pile near one of the goal posts.

The other team kicked off and got it deep before Skye intercepted a pass and dribbled all the way upfield. Just as she positioned herself to shoot, Bunk cut her off and knocked her away from the ball. She was much smaller, but she came right back at him, fighting for possession. She was *good*. *She* was the natural. Josh wondered how she'd gotten picked last.

Mark was a different story. Even after he tore himself away from the leaves, he spent more of his time watching than playing. He could run, but he looked kind of uncoordinated, and he treated the soccer ball like a curiosity, dancing around it, orbiting it like a distant planet. After Bunk shouted at him one more time, he wandered off the field, picked up his camera, and began snapping pictures. He moved up and down the sideline, standing, stooping, down on a knee. He returned to the field, got down on his elbows, and snapped off some photos of the leaves.

"What are you doin', Sillycorn?" Bunk yelled. "You're supposed to be playing defense."

Corey laughed. "Sillycorn!" he roared. "I like that. You're better off without him, Bunk."

In between long looks at the sky—for what, snow?—Mark kept taking pictures. He ignored the soccer players.

The rest of the game was scoreless, although Corey kept trying to pass the ball to Josh. Skye was battling it out with Bunk again as the bell rang.

"Afternoon recess?" Corey asked Josh as

they neared the school building.

"Sure," Josh said.

"What about hockey?" Corey said. "Do you play?"

"We don't have much hockey in Seattle."

"We do here," Bunk said. "Street hockey in the summer, ice hockey in the winter. It's awesome."

"I've got inline skates," Josh said.

"Me, too," Corey said. "But ice hockey's the best."

"Where's the ice?"

"The kids around here go to Poor Rooney's Pond," Corey said.

A weird name for a pond, Josh thought, but then what kind of name was *Bunk?* "I saw a lake. There wasn't any ice."

"Not yet. But it won't be long," Bunk said.

"I don't have ice skates."

"They've got good hockey skates in Coeur d'Alene for eighty or ninety bucks," Corey said. "Cheap. I bet your dad would get 'em for you."

"Maybe." But Josh doubted it. Eighty or ninety bucks didn't sound cheap.

"Talk to him," Corey said. "You'd be a natural. And we need an enforcer out there—somebody with some size."

Some *size*. Some *size* sounded better than some *fat*. Josh made up his mind. He would talk to his parents. He might be a natural.

This day was going better than he ever could have dreamed.

❄ 3 ❄
Student Council President

"Corey's just being nice to you because your dad's the high school coach," Skye whispered to Josh when he got back to their table.

"Why would he care what my dad does?"

"He thinks he's a star basketball player. And he'll be at the high school in a few years."

"So?"

"So it would help him to be buddy-buddy with the coach's kid."

"Maybe he just likes me," Josh said. "Did you think of that?"

"Not really," Skye said.

Mark laughed, loud enough to attract stares. Josh felt his face getting warm. "A river flows only downhill," Mark said. "Ask the fish."

What did that mean? Yes? No? Josh couldn't tell from the vacant expression on Mark's face, or the blank stare forming in his eyes. He was about to ask when he heard a wave of voices —hushed but excited—rise at the windows and roll over the classroom. Ms. Murphy held up her hand for silence, but murmurs kept swirling around the room. It was starting to snow.

Mark pulled something out of his backpack and unrolled it. It was a hat, a floppy one with a brim all around the crown, the kind fishermen wear. He put it on the table, right in front of him, keeping it close.

The excitement died down a bit, heads stopped turning, as the flakes kept falling. *Sticking or not sticking?* was the question. "You going fishing?" Josh asked Mark.

"I don't like snow," Mark whispered. "I don't like it falling on me. I might have to call my mother to come and get me." He fingered his hat and lifted it up to his head. Was he going to put it on?

"Everybody likes snow," Josh said.

"Mark doesn't," Skye said. She smiled at Mark. He returned the hat to the table.

Ms. Murphy explained a weekly assignment called "State Stats" to Josh and Mark. They had to turn in reports and maps for two states—West Virginia and Kentucky—by Wednesday. The first day at school, and homework had already started.

The snow stopped, leaving no trace on the ground. Mark lost his nervous look. Afternoon recess—twenty minutes of freedom—arrived, but Mark stayed inside. Ms. Murphy told him they needed to talk about something.

Outside, Corey and Bunk quickly chose sides for another soccer game. This time Bunk had the first pick, and he used it to take Josh. Skye ended up on Josh's team again. Halfway through the game, she dribbled around Corey and scored with a rocket shot off her left foot. The next time she got downfield, Corey knocked her to the ground, booted the ball upfield, then stood over her, laughing. She bounced up, glasses crooked, face dirty, and ran back to her position, but Josh saw tears in her eyes.

"If you can't take it, don't play!" Corey shouted after her. Bunk laughed, Alex laughed. Skye played harder. She went back to defense, and nothing got past her. Josh didn't score, but he had some chances, mostly on passes from Bunk.

Back in the classroom, Skye threw herself

into her chair, red-faced, eyes on fire.

"Why are you and Corey so friendly?" Josh asked her.

"He hates me. Ever since my first day at Mountain View, when I scored a goal against him, and smiled about it." Skye lowered her voice as several kids turned to look. "I don't care if he's student council president and whatever else he thinks he is, he's the biggest jerk in the school. A spoiled brat. A bully. He always has to be the best, especially around girls."

"Go to Ms. Murphy," Mark said. "She listens to us little people. Give her a crown and she'd be a princess."

"I did—last month. She suggested this mediation thing the school has."

"We had that at my old school," Josh said. "Another kid gets picked to help settle a fight. You have like a get-together with everybody."

"What happened?" Mark asked Skye.

"Ms. Murphy arranged this meeting with me, Corey, and a junior high girl. He faked his way through it, and he was okay for a couple of days, but then he took off the smiley-face mask. He was worse than ever. 'Wait till we're in junior high,' he told me, 'then you'll really be in for it.'"

Josh tried to imagine what Corey had planned for her. Nothing, he decided. Big talk, period. Skye just rubbed Corey the wrong way. "Tell your parents."

"*Parent*. My mom's in California with her new husband. My dad spends most of his time trying to get over her, trying to pretend everything's okay. He tries so hard, and he's worried about his new job. I can't tell him everything's not okay. I have to figure this out myself."

Mark frowned at his hands, knotted together on the table in front of him. He didn't look up when he talked. "The principal," he said. "Go to the school principal. Mrs. Drager?"

Skye shook her head. "They don't call her 'The Dragon' for nothing. They say she quit teaching because she can't stand kids. That she became a principal this year so she could hide out in her office. 'Don't go into the Dragon's Lair,' everyone says. Anyway, you can't get past Mrs. Benedict."

Skye looked like she was going to cry, and for a moment Josh felt sorry for her.

But not real sorry. Corey wasn't so bad. "Maybe you just need to quit bugging him," he said.

"Do you have something to contribute to

the class, Josh?" Ms. Murphy asked.

Heads turned, Josh swallowed, Skye frowned, Mark stared at his hands.

"No," Josh said.

"That's for sure," Skye whispered.

The faces turned to the front of the room. Josh settled back in his chair, trying to put on a smile, trying to smile inside. He was having a good day, way better than he'd expected. He wasn't going to think about anything else.

❄4❄
Christmas Is Coming

Outside the school entrance, past the school buses, past the sign that said WELCOME TO MOUNTAIN VIEW ELEMENTARY, sat Corey and Bunk. They were perched on a low cement wall, putting on their inline skates. Corey yelled, "Hey, Joshster! We're practicing up for the ice!" He gave Josh a thumbs-up sign and smiled.

Josh waved. Corey and Bunk got to their feet, shrugged on their backpacks, and skated out of the parking lot and across the street. Josh watched as they turned at the next street and headed toward Rathdrum Mountain.

"Your buddies leave you behind?" Skye had walked up quietly behind him. Mark stood at her side, looking up at the sky. Josh felt the needle in her words, but he was glad to hear them, anyway. He wanted to be her friend.

"They're not my buddies. Exactly."

"You're right," she said. "They won't be thinking of you on their little skate home."

"Don't you have to catch a bus?" Josh asked her. The needle was starting to sting.

"I'm a walker," she said.

"Me, too," Mark said.

"Where do you guys live?" Josh asked.

"Right over there," she said. "Sunlight Acres."

"Yeah?" Josh said. "That's where I live."

"I know. I saw you shooting baskets in your driveway yesterday."

"Oh."

"I live on Baxter Road," Mark said. "I've practiced the route." He closed his eyes. "Left, right, left, medium straight, right, left, long straight, left. Home."

"Baxter?" Skye said. "That's way on the other side of the development. That's bus rider distance."

Mark wrinkled his nose. "Buses smell. Buses have big windows and no seat belts."

"They're used to walking in Minnesota," Josh said. "When they're not riding snowmobiles."

"I don't ride snowmobiles—they don't

have roofs," Mark said. "Snow falls right on you." He checked the clouds again while Skye pulled a small, scuffed-up soccer ball from her backpack and dropped it at her feet. Without looking down, she smoothly boomeranged the ball from foot to foot, juggled it a couple of times, and sandwiched it against the grass with the sole of her shoe.

"What's that for?" Josh said.

"Practice," Skye said. "Getting better."

They crossed the street, then another. Mark seemed to be sticking to a map he had in his head, no meandering. Before they turned into Sunlight Acres, Josh looked toward the mountain. He could see Corey and Bunk—tiny, now—in the distance, skating along the shoulder of the road.

They walked past Josh's house, Skye still dribbling. He had to go to the Sinclairs', three houses away, so Mrs. Sinclair could keep an eye on him until either his mom or dad came home.

"I'm just in the next block," Skye said, pointing toward more rows of houses. "Maybe we could kick the soccer ball around sometime."

"I'd like that," Josh said.

"You, too," she said to Mark.

"I have studies," he said, eyes down.

"I didn't mean today," she said. "Just sometime." They stopped in front of the Sinclairs'.

"I have studies," Mark repeated. "And so it goes. And so I go." He hurried off, looking at the sidewalk, not looking back.

Josh raised his eyebrows at Skye, expecting a comment on Mark's weird behavior. Instead, she turned and watched him disappear down the street, then looked back at Josh. She jammed her hands in her sweatshirt pockets and stood, not moving, sad-eyed behind her glasses, one foot anchoring her soccer ball to the sidewalk, as if she wasn't eager to get home.

"You miss your mom?" Josh asked. The question sounded stupid to him, but it was already out.

"She's been gone almost a year," Skye answered. "Dad got custody."

Josh studied her face, waiting.

"Every day," she added. "Even when I've visited, when I'm *with* her, I miss her. I know she's not coming back."

Josh tried to think of something comforting to say. "Sorry," he said finally. "I bet that's awful."

She sighed and smiled a thin smile.

"I guess I'm lucky," he continued lamely. "My parents get in arguments sometimes, but

41

they always tell me not to worry, that they couldn't afford to get a divorce. It's their idea of humor."

Skye smiled wider. It was good to see. She raised her hand in the air and he high-fived her. "Hooray for poor parents," she said. She backed away, still smiling, then turned and started for home, dribbling quicker now.

"See you tomorrow," Josh said.

"Okay, Rookie," she called back.

❅ ❅ ❅

At dinner that night, Josh told the family about his day. They wanted to hear about school, his teacher, his classmates, but he hurried through that stuff. He wanted to talk about soccer, about getting chosen first, about scoring a goal, about Corey and Bunk. He told them about Skye and how good she was at soccer, about Mark being afraid of snow. But most of all Josh wanted to talk about ice skating, about hockey skates.

"Christmas is coming," his dad said.

"These guys want me to play *soon*," Josh said. "They like me."

"Lots of people like you, Josh," his mom said.

"But these guys are seventh-graders," he said. "*Popular* seventh-graders."

"Christmas isn't that far off," his mom

said. "Thanksgiving's practically here."

"Skates are only eighty dollars," Josh said. He thought his mom would be more on his side. Wasn't she glad he was making new friends?

"Do *you* have that kind of money?" Josh's dad said.

"Not right now."

"We're glad you've made some new friends," his mom said, "and we want you to be able to do things with them..." Her voice trailed off. Josh waited for the *but*.

"Hockey's a tough sport," his dad said. "It would take a lot of practice to get good at it. And you haven't exactly worked hard at the other things you've tried."

Josh thought of the other sports—basketball, baseball, football (not track, not with his body)—his dad had dangled in front of him. He thought of all the underused equipment gathering dust somewhere. But maybe hockey really *would* be his sport. "This would be different," he said.

"Well, Christmas is coming," his dad said. "But if you don't want to wait, we could come up with some jobs for you. We've got a fence to build, and there are tons of rocks that need to be mined out of that backyard before we can put in a lawn."

Josh wasn't sure he wanted the skates that bad. But how else would he get them in time? "Maybe I could try the rock mining."

"Let me know when," his dad said. "I'll show you what I want, and we can come up with a fair wage."

"Soon." Josh didn't say anything about the wage. He'd have to think about it. But he was sure his idea of fair wouldn't be in the same ballpark as his dad's. "Do you know where my inline skates are?"

"Probably in the garage," his dad said. "The box should be marked."

After dinner Josh went to the garage and found his skates. He tried them on. They were a little snug, but he'd be able to go out and practice tomorrow after school.

When he finally went to bed, he had a hard time falling asleep. Partly it was the unfamiliar surroundings, but mostly it was excitement. It was soccer. It was hockey and skates. It was new friends. It was guys who *liked* him for his size. It was all the things that had happened that day and all the things that might happen the next.

And it was one more thing: a little edgy feeling he tried to ignore. A little edgy feeling that something wasn't quite right.

❄5❄
Canaries

The sky was gray, the air chilly, when Josh walked outside the next morning. But there was no frost, no layer of ice on the puddles in the street. Maybe he wouldn't need those ice skates before Christmas.

"JOSH!" The voice carried through the still air as if it had come over a loudspeaker. He looked up the block to see Mark hurrying toward him.

"Hey, Mark," he said as they turned toward school. He glanced back, wondering about Skye. She was nowhere in sight.

"Hey," Mark said, not looking Josh in the face but instead staring at his right shoulder.

"Did you work on your state report last night?"

"I thought about it," Josh said.

"Did you know that Abraham Lincoln was born in Kentucky?"

"No." Josh didn't really care.

"Did you know that in Kentucky and West Virginia, men go deep into the earth to mine for coal?" Mark said.

"I've heard about that."

"It used to be a really dangerous job. There were cave-ins, and illnesses, and fires, and explosions. Do you know that old-time miners carried birds—canaries—in cages with them?"

"Why?" Now Josh was curious.

"Coal gas. If there was a leak of coal gas into the mine, the canaries would be the first ones affected. They'd die, then the men would know they had to get out."

"The canaries died?"

"To save the men."

"They probably thought the men were just being nice to them, like going on a picnic or something." Josh pictured a little yellow bird in a wire cage, swinging on a trapeze, chirping cheerfully, then growing sleepy and toppling over.

"They were fooled," Mark said.

"I don't think birds have much of a brain."

"Watch out!" Suddenly Mark grabbed Josh's elbow and steered him around a freshly deposited dog pile in the middle of the sidewalk. Mark seemed to have a hard time looking at a person's face, but sometimes he saw things nobody else noticed.

"Why do you like Corey and Bunk?" Mark asked.

Mark was full of questions this morning. Josh thought for a minute. He wasn't sure he really did *like* them. But other kids must. Corey and Bunk were in the popular group, probably on top of it. Anyway, he could be in their little circle without being *like* them. He could still be himself. "They're pretty cool guys," he said. "For Rathdrum, anyway."

"Cool?"

"Yeah. You just need to be cooler around them and they'll like you, too. Don't say stuff that makes Corey mad. Laugh when he says something funny. Pass him the ball when he's on your team. Don't show him up when he isn't."

"If I could show him up, I would," Mark said. "I'd be like Skye, under his skin like a tick. But I'm not good at sports. I don't like sports. Even if I did, I don't want to play with that bully. He's mean to Skye. I'll be the official photographer. I'm better at photography."

"Skye's asking for trouble. All we have to do is make it through this year, be nice to the big guys, then next year we'll rule."

"Be nice to Corey and Bunk?" Mark said. "You will walk into a room and people will think of the droppings of dogs."

Josh shook his head. "They're not that bad."

"To know the road ahead," Mark said, "ask those coming back." Another of Mark's little sayings. Josh had an idea what this one meant: Mark had already been down the road with Corey.

They didn't talk the rest of the way. When they got to the school grounds, Corey and Bunk were sitting out front, taking off their skates, putting them in their backpacks.

"The *Joshster*," Corey said. Josh stopped, Mark kept on going. "Don't go away mad, *Sillycorn*, just go away," Corey said to Mark's back. Corey snickered, and Bunk joined in. Alex walked up, eating a candy bar and smiling, although he'd arrived too late to know why Corey and Bunk were laughing.

"Gimme that," Corey said to Alex, who handed over the candy. Corey took a big bite from the uneaten end, chewed, swallowed, belched, and threw the rest toward a garbage can. It bounced off and landed on the grass. "Pick it up," he growled at Alex, and Alex did. But his eyes got glassy. He wiped at them as he turned and started for the school.

Josh felt his insides knot up. He thought about what Mark had just said—about those coming back. What would Alex have to say about Corey?

"Did you talk to your parents about the skates, Josh buddy?" Corey said.

"Maybe for Christmas, they told me."

"Hey, you'll miss out on a whole month of skating," Bunk said.

"I found my street skates," Josh said. "I can practice on those."

"It's just not the same, Joshster." Corey reached into his jacket pocket. "Look."

Josh stepped close as Corey held up a photo: five kids, smiling, dressed for the cold in thick parkas. They wore ice skates; they held hockey sticks by their sides like trophy fish. They stood on a sheet of smooth white ice that stretched behind them to a steep, chalky shoreline shadowed by dark pines heavy with snow. It was Corey and Bunk and three other seventh-graders Josh had seen at recess.

"Poor Rooney's Pond," Corey said. "Last winter. What do you think?"

Josh's heart filled with longing. "Awesome."

"You can be there, man," Bunk said.

"You just gotta get those parents to spring for the skates," Corey said.

"Maybe I can earn the money."

"That would take too long," Corey said. "We'll have ice soon. You don't want to miss the first time out there. Maybe you could owe it to 'em. You know, work it off later."

"Maybe." The backyard rock project didn't seem like such a chore now.

"Do it," Bunk ordered, and Josh felt the words like a surprise knee to the chest. They took his breath away.

Corey gave Bunk a look, then smiled at Josh. "The more the merrier, Joshster." His grin turned to a frown as his eyes shifted from Josh's face to a spot somewhere past Josh's shoulder. Josh followed his gaze: fifty feet away, Skye—head down, jaw set—was making a beeline for the double doors. Josh looked back at Corey, who stared at her, cold-eyed, until she was inside.

"You really think I could play?" Josh said, trying to distract Corey—for a few minutes, at least—from whatever thoughts he was having about Skye.

"No doubt, Josh buddy. I've seen you on the soccer field, remember?"

Josh didn't think he'd been that impressive, but he'd try to trust Corey on this one. "Yeah."

Corey held up the photo. "You could be in this picture next time."

Josh nodded. He looked down, where his jeans were bunched up at his ankles. He imagined himself light on his feet, rocketing across the ice on shiny new hockey skates with flashing blades.

"Want to go see it?" Corey jerked his head toward the mountain. "We'll take you out there. You can look at it yourself."

"When?"

"After school. Or before. Anytime you can go."

"It's less than a mile," Bunk said. "Fifteen minutes walking."

The bell rang, and they started for the doors. "Maybe I can."

"You gotta see it," Corey said. "Talk to your parents."

The sky failed to shed any snow that morning. On the way out to lunch recess, Alex hurried to catch Josh. "You're gonna get skates?" he asked.

"I hope so."

"You've got to. It's so cool out at the pond."

"I hate hockey," Skye said. She and Mark had come out behind them. "It's just an excuse to go crashing into people."

"I can't wait," Alex said.

Josh thought of Corey's photo; he pictured his face in the middle of it. He looked at Skye and Mark. "You guys should come, too."

"Will Corey be there?" Mark said, staring past Alex's face.

"He's the man," Alex said.

"NOT ME," Mark said.

They got to the soccer field. Corey and Bunk chose sides again. They started play. Josh got a dead-on pass from Corey but muffed the wide-open shot. Corey shrugged as if he didn't care, but his face hardened. He spit at the dirt. Josh's insides flip-flopped as he struggled to get back upfield, feeling clumsy and heavy.

Skye raced in from the wing and scored for Bunk's team despite Corey's attempt to take her down with a wicked slide tackle from the side.

Mark, watching from the sidelines, snapping off pictures, giving a nonstop play-by-play of the action on the field, grew louder. "AND SKYE SPRINTS IN. SHE ELUDES COREY'S VICIOUS TACKLE AND RACES BY HIM WITH THE BALL DANCING AT HER FEET. SHE DRIVES THE BALL

PAST THE HELPLESS DIVING GOALIE AND SCORES."

Skye laughed. Corey got up, muddy, and stormed after her. "Shut up, Sillycorn!" he yelled at Mark. For the rest of the game, Corey didn't play a position. Wherever Skye was, he was, shouldering her off the ball, pushing, tripping, shoving her to the ground. But she didn't give up.

Mark kept up the play-by-play. "THE OPPONENTS RESORT TO DIRTY PLAY, BUT SKYE REFUSES TO WILT. SHE'S EVERYWHERE, A THORN IN COREY'S SIDE."

"Can't take it, Sillycorn?" Corey said as the game ended and they started for the school. "Gotta stand on the sidelines like a little girlie cheerleader?"

"Why do you bother Skye?"

"*She* bothers me. And so do you. Any more of the sports announcer act and you'll be chewing on dirt."

"She does nothing to you. You should stop troubling her."

"You gonna, like, *make* me, twerp?"

"I can take care of myself," Skye said. Her jeans and sweatshirt were caked with mud, but she didn't seem to notice. Josh watched her jaw tighten; he felt his throat doing the same.

"Sure you can, Skye," Corey said. "For *now*."

Skye stopped in her tracks; Mark stayed with her. Corey, Bunk, and Alex walked on. Josh felt stretched, then torn. He took a few steps and slowed to a stop, watching the three guys continue on toward the entrance.

Corey turned. "See ya', Josh buddy," he said, and Josh gave a feeble wave at their backs.

"Why didn't you go with 'em, *Josh buddy*?" Skye said.

"He sees what they are," Mark said, holding his nose.

Josh thought of that morning on the way to school, the dog poop. He imagined people sniffing the air when he walked into a room with Corey and Bunk's smell on him.

"The *Joshster*?" Skye said. "He thinks they're *cool*. He's their *friend*."

"Not really," Josh said. "They just think I'm good at sports." At least they used to. He wasn't so sure now. Maybe he'd be able to redeem himself once the pond iced over, once he got his skates. All the time he'd spent on street skates would have to help. He hoped.

"You should go to Mrs. Drager," Mark said to Skye. "Corey is harassing you."

"I couldn't get past her guard dog," Skye said. "And it would just be my word against his."

"I could go with you," Mark said to her, but his eyes were on his camera. "Two voices."

"Thanks," Skye said. "I'll think about it." She gave Mark a smile, wide and warm, and Josh wondered what *he* could do to earn that smile again.

Besides a trip to the principal, that is. He wasn't ready to go to the Dragon's Lair. Corey acted like a bully sometimes, but he hadn't picked on Josh. Corey was Josh's ticket to popularity. If Skye and Mark could just figure out a way to get on Corey's good side, Josh wouldn't have to make a choice he didn't want to make.

He wouldn't have to feel as if he were standing on a train station platform, cold to the bone, trying to decide between two trains heading off in opposite directions, wanting to get on both, not wanting to wave good-bye to either.

Weight

"Where on Baxter Road do you live?" Skye asked Mark. She toed her little soccer ball ahead of her on the sidewalk. Josh was barely listening as the three of them headed toward the entrance to Sunlight Acres. He didn't know Baxter Road from bath water. The wind on his face was cold enough to make his eyes hurt. The air smelled different from Seattle air; it smelled like snow. Once again his mind was on those skates and how he could get them—fast.

"The Baxter farm," Mark said.

"The old Baxter place?" Skye said, and Josh's ears perked up. He liked his new house, but something about living on a farm called "the old Baxter place" sounded a lot more interesting.

"I heard about it from the librarian after we moved in last summer," Skye continued. "She said it's historical. I didn't think anyone lived there."

"It was vacant when we moved in," Mark said.

"I've been past it a lot," Skye said. "Big white house, red barn, even a silo. It looks cool."

"Do you think we could see it sometime?" Josh said.

Mark smiled at the bare limbs of a tree. "Sometime, maybe."

"How about today?" Skye said. "I don't have piano or anything on Tuesdays."

"Today?" Mark's voice rose. "REALLY?"

"I'll just have to ask my dad," Skye said.

"Me, too," Josh said. "I'll have to call my mom or dad from the Sinclairs'."

Mark nodded. "Okay." But he looked worried.

They stopped at the Sinclairs', where Josh called and got permission from his mom to walk to Mark's house if he promised to be back by 5:00. At Skye's house they met her dad, a reporter for the *Coeur d'Alene Press*, who looked them over closely and asked some reporterlike questions before saying yes.

At the back entrance to Sunlight Acres they turned west, toward Rathdrum Mountain.

They walked along the shoulder of a highway, past fields with horses and cattle and sheep and even a pair of llamas. A black-and-white sheep dog with no tail raced out from a barn to the wire fence and kept pace with them until they came to a sign that said Baxter Road.

"Left," Mark announced, and they took a left, onto a road that wound through a thick stand of pine trees, and walked until the road turned to gravel. When they came out of the trees, the wind, unchecked, pressed against them like cold hands. At the top of a small rise, Mark slowed and pointed.

"There," he said, and Skye nodded. Off to their left, set well back from the road, stood a tall white house surrounded by a big patch of brown grass and clumps of scrubby green pines. Behind the house sat a red barn, badly in need of paint, and a wooden silo the same color and condition. They turned down the dirt driveway, past the remains of a rail fence.

Mark opened the back door and motioned for Josh and Skye to come in. They went through a big kitchen and dining room and ended up at the bottom of a staircase near the front door.

"MOTHER!" Mark's voice filled the whole

entryway, bouncing off the wood floor and bare walls.

Josh heard a voice, then footsteps, from overhead. A moment later Mark's mom appeared on the upstairs landing.

"We're here," Mark said.

"And who is 'we'?" Mark's mom smiled that big shiny smile as she came down the stairs. Josh was glad to see it; Mark hadn't given her any warning about visitors. "Are you going to introduce your friends, Mark?"

"My mother," Mark said, glancing at the floor, the wall, the ceiling, everywhere but at her. "Skye and Josh. From school."

"I remember Josh," Mark's mom said, her eyes glowing with blue fire. "It's good to see you again. And it's very nice to meet you, Skye. I love your name."

"Thank you," Skye said.

Josh, then Skye, shook her hand. Her grip was warm.

"May we go upstairs?" Mark said.

"Of course," his mom said.

Mark's room was toasty, despite the big windows and high ceilings. A twin bed and small dresser were on one side, a desk on the other. Unlike Josh's bed at home, this one looked as if it had never been slept in. The dark blue bedspread, dotted with stars and planets, was stretched tight as a drum skin over the bed. The pillow was fluffed up and perfectly centered at the head.

"You sleep on the floor or something?" Josh said.

Mark smiled. "On the bed."

"Your mom make it for you?"

"She taught me, but I make it. I like my room neat."

Josh eyed the bed. He thrummed his fingers against the spread, feeling the vibrations. "You get up a half-hour early just to make your bed?"

"It takes forty-three seconds, on average."

Skye whistled. "How do you do it?"

"I sleep on top of the covers," Mark said. "I wear my sweats."

"Just so you don't mess up your bed?" Josh said.

"Not entirely," Mark said.

"What then?" Josh said.

"There's the weight problem," Mark said.

Josh waited for an explanation.

"Weight problem?" Skye said.

Mark bounced up and down on the polished wood floor. It whispered a series of creaks. "We're on the second story," he said. "This house is a hundred years old."

"So?" Josh said.

"If there's too much weight up here, the floor could collapse," Mark said.

"Oh." Josh felt as if he'd slipped into a place where everyday words had a different meaning. "What's that got to do with you sleeping on top of your covers?"

Mark smiled a patient smile. "Weight," he said. "If the covers are on top of me, I'll weigh more. Maybe too much. I could cause the bed to crash right through the floor."

"But—" Josh began.

"The floor feels real solid," Skye said, kindly. She knelt down and rapped it with her knuckles. She went into a crouch and leaped high and landed flat-footed. "Barely a creak," she said.

Mark edged toward his desk. Worried eyes and a curious smile fought for control of his face. He pulled his camera from his backpack and aimed it at Skye. "Do that again."

"What?"

"Knock on the floor. Jump high and land hard."

"Is there film in the camera?" she said.

"It's digital."

"Okay." She bent and knocked on the floor until Mark had snapped off half a dozen photos. She crouched and leaped once and again and again while he clicked away.

"Thank you," he said.

"Want me to do it now?" Josh said.

Frowning, Mark looked Josh up and down. "The knocking," he said softly. His face colored a little. "Not the leaping—you're too...big. Please."

"No problem." Josh bent down and rapped firmly on the floorboards and smiled at the camera while Mark took more pictures. The floor was stout. Mark could have had a collection of barnyard animals visit his room without it collapsing.

Mark's mom poked her head into the room. "How is it?" she asked Josh, as if testing Mark's bedroom floor was the most normal thing in the world. As if taking pictures of the event was an expected part of everyday life.

"Good," Josh said. "Rock-solid."

"And you have the pictures, Mark," she said to him.

"Yes."

She smiled and left.

Carefully Mark set the camera on his desk, as if its weight might be a problem. On the desk, sandwiched between piles of videotapes and DVDs and stacks of books, sat a computer. Next to the desk was a tall cabinet with a TV, VCR, DVD player, and stereo system. Its radio, the source of the voices Josh had heard, was tuned to NPR, Josh's parents' favorite station. "You listen to that?" he asked Mark, who held up a finger to signal quiet. A woman on the radio was saying something about an interview with a scientist scheduled for the next day. Mark grabbed a note pad from his desk and scribbled down the time.

"Wonderful information," he said.

"No music," Josh said.

"Sometimes there is."

Josh made a face. Opera, probably. He picked up a thick, heavy book and looked at the cover: *Minerals of North America*. He set it back down on another bruiser: *The Field Guide to Pacific Northwest Wildlife*. Not exactly page-turners. Then he spotted *Bigfoot and Other Unusual Phenomena: A Scientific Approach*. He wouldn't mind cracking open that one. "Have you read all these books?"

"Not at the same time."

Outside the windows, where life still seemed normal, dusk was settling in. Josh looked at his watch. "I've gotta get going."

"Me, too, I guess," Skye said.

"Can you stay a few more minutes?" Mark said, his eyes focused on the empty space between them. "We have cookies from the store.

It's a big package."

"Okay," Josh said. He did have a few minutes. And as usual, he was hungry.

As they started down the stairs, he heard the woman on the radio say that a cold front was expected to move into eastern Washington and northern Idaho. Soon.

They downed cookies and milk sitting at a wooden table in the big kitchen. They were nearly done when Josh heard the front door open and close. A moment later a man came into the room. He wore a dark gray suit, a white shirt, and a blue-and-gray striped tie. His black shoes reflected the glow from the ceiling light. He set a grocery bag on the counter and smiled at Mark.

"Hey, Marky," he said. He had a gentle, bedtime-story voice. He came over and gave Mark a big hug. Mark stiffened. The man smiled at Skye, then Josh. "Are you going to introduce us, Marky?" he said.

Mark leveled his eyes at the man's chest. "Skye and Josh, this is my dad."

Mark's dad reached out to shake hands with Skye, then Josh. He looked them in the eye. "Nice to meet both of you," he said, and they told him it was nice to meet him, too. "I hope you'll come back and visit us again," he said. He sounded as if he meant it. "I know this house is a little off the beaten path, but we like it. And there's plenty of room to play." Josh remembered Mark saying that his dad's job was helping people. Josh could imagine him doing that, but what kind of helping would it be?

Mr. Silverthorn left the room. Josh and Skye finished their snack, then Mark walked them to the road. The gray day had changed to charcoal when Josh and Skye turned at the gate and waved at Mark. He waved back, but his eyes, glowing in the twilight, looked off at some trees. Josh felt comforted and uncomfortable at the same time. He liked Mark, but what was up with him?

"Weird kid," Josh said.

"He's not that much different from us."

"You, maybe," Josh said. "I'm not afraid snow might fall on my head. I look people in the face when I'm talking to them. When my dad hugs me, I hug him back. I don't do play-by-play on kids' soccer games. Then there's Mark's bed. The 'weight problem'? Does that make any sense? How about taking pictures of people testing a floor that would probably hold up under a herd of cows? How about the way he talks, like a short grownup?"

"I'd choose Mark over your buddies."

"They're not my buddies."

"You're right," Skye said. "They're trouble."

"Not for me."

"For everybody. Corey wants something from you."

"I don't have anything he wants."

"You think he'd even be talking to you if you weren't the coach's kid?"

Skye wasn't looking for an answer, he knew, but he wanted to say YES, loud enough to drown out the noise of his own doubts. "Why do you care?"

She smiled a little smile that he barely caught in the early-evening gloom. "I don't really know—maybe because rookies have to stick together."

❄ 7 ❄
Just Another Kid

The cold front arrived the next day, Wednesday. Not bitter, yet, but biting. A lumpy quilt of gunmetal gray clouds hung low over the valley as Josh stepped outside. To the east sunrise was barely a promise, but still, in that dim light, he noticed a shimmer of ice on the puddles in the street.

On the way to school, Mark seemed nervous. He kept looking up at the sky, as if he expected it to fall on his head. He wore the hat with the wrap-around brim. At his side he clutched a big white-and-green-striped golf umbrella. He fingered the release button, ready to press it at the first sign of trouble.

Before the bell rang, Ms. Murphy called the three of them up to her desk. Special attention from a teacher made Josh nervous. He wondered what kind of trouble they were in.

"This afternoon I'm going to make an announcement," Ms. Murphy said. "I'm going to tell everyone that we're going to change the seating arrangements. We'll have at least two kids from each table move to different ones."

"Why?" Josh was just getting settled in. He liked where he was. He liked being with Skye and Mark.

"I think change is good for the dynamics of the class, Josh," Ms. Murphy said. "But the reason I brought you three up here is to tell you I'd like you to stay together."

Mark looked out the windows, grinning. Josh nodded, relieved.

Skye smiled. She looked curious. "Why?"

"Mark and I have already talked about this," Ms. Murphy said. Mark looked at the floor, the clock on the wall, the ceiling. His face colored. "Why don't you stay behind for a few minutes when the class goes to lunch, Skye? You too, Josh. We can take as much time as you want to talk."

And miss lunch recess? "It's okay," Josh said. "I want to stay together."

"So do I," Skye said.

"We need to talk," Ms. Murphy said, "anyway."

68

When the lunch bell rang, Mark was the last to leave, glancing over his shoulder as he walked out the classroom door.

"You asked why I was keeping you together," Ms. Murphy said. "And it's a fair question. If one of your classmates asks, it's because you're just getting to know each other. But the real reason is that sometimes life gives us an opportunity to help someone. Even if we aren't looking for the opportunity." She looked back and forth between Josh and Skye, studying their faces.

Skye was nodding, as if she knew something.

"You two have only known each other for a few days," Ms. Murphy said. "You haven't known Mark any longer. But I've watched the three of you together. I've watched the way you act around him. I like what I see. I like the way you treat him like just another kid."

"He's not?" Skye said.

"Skye thought he was," Josh said.

"You thought he was a freak," Skye said.

"I didn't say that."

Ms. Murphy held up her hand, controlling the traffic of words. "Do you like him, Josh?"

"Yeah. He's just different. He likes different stuff. He acts different."

"Unique," Skye said.

"Exactly," Ms. Murphy said. "Unique. Exceptional. Like a lot of kids—and adults—Mark has some exceptional needs. We want to do our best to meet them. The school—the teachers and other people who work here—will do what it can. But it's just as important for his schoolmates to do what they can, probably more so."

"That's where we come in?" Skye said.

"Yes. I know it's asking a lot, but if you already consider him your friend, maybe you won't think of this as such a burden. What I want you to do is be there for Mark, sit with him, listen to him, give him your support, overlook his differences while at the same time accommodating them. Keep treating him as if he's a regular Joe."

"Be his friend," Josh said.

"And more," Ms. Murphy said. "You'll learn things from Mark that you could never learn from an everyday kid."

"Why's he so—?" Josh began.

"Eccentric," Skye finished for him, but that wasn't exactly what he was thinking. He was thinking goofy, but not a bad kind of goofy.

"Mark asked that this not go beyond you two," Ms. Murphy said. "Can you honor that request?"

Josh and Skye nodded in unison.

"Good," Ms. Murphy said. "Have either of you heard of autism?"

"I saw something on TV about it," Skye said, and Josh thought that he had, too. Kids who lived in their own world. They didn't listen or talk or act like they knew anyone else was around. "Closed-door kids," Skye continued. "Something's going on inside them, but no one knows what."

"Exactly," Ms. Murphy said. "Sometimes something surprising comes out."

"That's not Mark," Josh said.

"No and yes," Ms. Murphy said. "Mark has a very mild form of autism. Kids—and adults—who have this kind of autism can communicate. They can learn and think, sometimes brilliantly. But they don't do these things the way most of us do. Some experts say they think in pictures instead of words."

Josh thought about Mark's camera. Was this thinking-in-pictures thing the reason Mark was so interested in photography?

"This autism Mark has," Skye said. "What's it called?"

"It has a long name," Ms. Murphy said. "Asperger syndrome."

"You don't have to worry about me remembering that," Josh said.

Ms. Murphy smiled. "You won't be tested on it."

"Do his parents know?' Skye said.

"They've known for a long time. They've seen him make progress, including friendships, at his last school. We want to make sure his gains continue."

"Thanks for telling us," Skye said, sitting a little taller.

"So what do you think?" Ms. Murphy said.

"I think we have an opportunity," Skye said.

Josh stood. "Rookies rule," he said. "Let's eat lunch."

By the time Josh and Skye had eaten, recess was winding down. And it looked even colder outside. They decided to walk to the library, taking their time down the long hallway.

"Do you think Mark knows what Ms. Murphy told us?" Josh said.

"She got his okay, so he knows she told us something. Maybe that he's a little different. That he has some problems."

"I guess," Josh said. He hoped Mark didn't feel like a sideshow attraction. Josh remembered how his friend Little Joe had been stared at and talked about and teased just because he was short.

Back at the classroom, it was moving time for nearly everyone but the rookies. They got a few looks from other kids, but no one asked why they weren't being stirred into the new mixture.

A few minutes after everyone settled into their places, the gray-haired teacher Josh had seen in the office on his first day came to the classroom door. She had a short, quiet conversation with Ms. Murphy, then Ms. Murphy came over and asked Mark to go with the woman for a while.

"Clock repair," Mark said under his breath as he got up to leave.

❀ ❀ ❀

On the way home, Mark wore his fisherman hat, pulled low against the wind and cold. He had his umbrella ready.

"Expecting snow?" Josh said.

"Soon, I think," Mark said. "Snow, soon. And ice. And cold that will test your heart."

❊ 8 ❊
Poor Rooney's Pond

Thanksgiving day passed quietly. Josh watched too much football, ate too much food, and sat around a lot. After dinner he skated up and down the street for a half-hour or so, but the cold drove him back inside.

When he went to bed that night, the weatherman on a Coeur d'Alene radio station was giving the report: continuing possibility of snow; twenty-three degrees and falling.

Friday came. More football on TV. More street skating. He dressed warmer against the deepening cold, and lasted longer. He felt more comfortable, lighter on his feet. He couldn't keep his mind off the pond and what it would be like to be out there on real hockey skates, showing Corey what he could do. He hoped.

In the afternoon, Josh worked on his homework and dug in the hard backyard, prospecting for rocks. He got in a couple tough hours, a couple piles of rocks, but at four dollars an hour, the pay he and his dad had settled on, it was going to be a long while before he would earn enough for a pair of skates.

Snow fell overnight, an inch or so of white. On Saturday morning the clouds cleared away, and Josh, sore-handed, went to the garage to reunite himself with the shovel. But the yard was crusty with new snow and with frost that had reached even farther down to form a stubborn shell of frozen dirt. He made another small pile of rocks, another four dollars, then gave up. He was miles from getting those skates.

Saturday afternoon the phone rang. Josh's dad called him to the kitchen.

"Joshster!" the voice on the phone said.

"Corey?"

"You got it, Josh buddy."

Something in Corey's voice reminded Josh of what Mark had said about the droppings of dogs. "What's going on?"

"*You.* I thought I'd check and see if you want to go out to the pond with me and take a look. I have a feeling there's some ice out there by now."

"Sure!"

"Good. Just head down the road like you're going to the Heights. We'll meet you."

"When?"

"How soon can you leave?"

Josh checked with his dad, then came back to the phone. "Five minutes."

"Great. We'll meet you in about fifteen."

Josh spotted Corey and Bunk as he walked up the long, gentle hill to Prairie Heights. They waved and motioned for him to follow them down a gravel side road. He caught up with them just past a dead end sign, where the road narrowed and curved into a dense grove of pines.

"The Joshster," Corey said, and punched him playfully on the shoulder. "How you doin', buddy?"

"Good."

"You didn't get any unexpected Thanksgiving gifts, did you?" Corey said. "Like a pair of skates, for instance?"

"Afraid not."

"Maybe Santa will come early," Corey said.

"Or the Easter Bunny," Bunk said.

Josh figured one was about as likely as the other. "Doubt it."

Light broke through the trees up ahead.

The road angled right, dead-ending into a clearing, and suddenly there it was. The pond. Almost like the picture, but not quite. The trees surrounding it were mostly free of snow, the ground showed through brown and green in patches, and the ice hadn't taken over. Not yet. It had worked its way out from the shoreline for forty feet or so, but the pond was big—an oval nearly the size of a football field. Its center, most of the pond, was still clear of ice, but the blue water looked thick and sluggish.

Corey whistled. "Won't be long now. Not in this weather."

They walked to the pond's edge, and Bunk kicked a small rock onto the ice. It bounced and skidded and plopped into the water. Josh imagined himself standing out on the frozen surface, skates on his feet, a hockey stick in his hand, posing for a picture, then taking off, blades flashing, for a run at the goal. His dad said hockey was a tough sport, but how hard could it be?

Corey picked up a bigger rock—baseball-size—and lobbed it onto the ice. Slivers of ice flew, but the rock didn't break through. It skipped to the edge and slipped off. "In a few days it'll survive a bomb blast," he said, grinning.

Josh wasn't sure about that.

He remembered a cold spell in Seattle and the signs at Green Lake warning people to stay off the ice. He'd heard stories about kids breaking through ice and drowning.

"How did it get its name?" he asked.

"Its name?" Corey said.

"You know—Poor Rooney's Pond."

"Who knows?" Corey said. "Maybe some guy who used to live around here was named Rooney. Maybe he was poor."

"Oh." Josh put one foot carefully on the ice, shifted his weight onto it, and felt lunch—a turkey sandwich—rise up in his stomach as the surface seemed to give. He backed off. The print of his shoe showed perfectly in the thin layer of snow. Corey, then Bunk, stepped on with both feet. Gingerly.

"Solid," Corey said, but he went no farther than the edge. Neither did Bunk. When they eased off the ice, they left four more prints, the size of Josh's but not as deep. He wished he'd gone easier on the Thanksgiving dinner and the leftovers and all the other junk he'd put away the last few days. He could feel the fat cells multiplying, pushing against the waist of his jeans like rising bread dough.

He looked up at the darkening sky. "I should get back."

"Us, too," Corey said. "But what do you think?"

"Awesome."

"You won't know how awesome till you try it," Corey said. "You'll be a star, man."

"Shining," Bunk said.

Josh wasn't sure. But he was pretty certain about one thing: he wanted to be out there. "I just need to get my skates."

Corey took off a glove and reached in his pocket. He pulled out a quarter and handed it to Josh. "Make a wish," he said, "and toss it in the pond."

Josh looked at the quarter, then at Corey, trying to decide if he was serious.

"Go ahead," Corey said. "Sometimes wishes come true."

Josh closed his eyes, picturing those skates, picturing them on his feet. He opened his eyes, stared out at that icy water, and threw the quarter. It landed far beyond the ice with a little plop, a barely visible splash.

"A natural," Corey said, and smiled.

When Josh got home, his dad was hanging a new thermometer outside the back door.

It read nineteen degrees.

❄ 9 ❄
Out of Control

Monday morning dawned, cold and threatening. Josh gulped down his cornflakes and toast, put on his hat, got his backpack, and went outside to wait for Skye and Mark. A thin layer of new snow covered the ground. He kicked at an icy puddle at the curb: frozen solid. He pictured Poor Rooney's Pond, thickening its ice just for him.

Skye and Mark arrived, puffs of breath mushrooming in front of their faces. Skye was dribbling her soccer ball, controlling it as if she had it tied to one of her feet. Mark carried his umbrella, ready to be popped open at the first sign of snow. Maybe to be extra-prepared, he had the hood of his bright yellow ski jacket up. But his eyes were down. As usual, he seemed to be taking peeks into his own curious world.

Skye dribbled ahead twenty feet or so. She turned and passed the ball back in Josh and Mark's direction. Mark avoided it the way he would a low-flying cannonball. He jogged ahead, a few steps beyond Skye. Josh trapped the ball and passed it back to her.

They moved on, a small parade, Mark leading the way. Skye came next, scuttling backwards, passing the ball back and forth to Josh. As they neared the corner, Josh noticed a silver-colored van approaching from far down the block to their left, engine humming, wheels slipping, going too fast for the icy road.

Mark must have seen it, too. He was looking in the direction of the van, flapping his arms up and down in a robotic, slow-down motion.

Josh heard voices. He heard footsteps. Suddenly three small kids, bundled up against the cold, jostling each other, raced past him and toward the corner.

"Stop!" Josh called.

Two of them did, before they got to Skye. But the third child, a boy with a blue stocking hat pulled low over his ears, seemed not to hear.

"Stop!" Josh shouted. The little kid looked

back, laughing, as he raced past Skye. He didn't see what was coming from down the street, but Mark had. He tried to grab the boy, but it was an awkward, off-balance try, and he missed.

The kid lurched into the street backwards.

Rubber slid dully against ice. The van swerved, then spun out of control, horn blaring, toward the boy. He stopped in the middle of the street, wide-eyed. He tried to scramble back but fell, face-down.

Josh froze. This was a dream. One of those dreams where something bad is happening, but you can't move to stop it.

Skye turned toward the scene behind her, a first paralyzing glimpse.

But Mark was closest to the action. And he must have had a picture in his head of what was coming. Because now he moved. He stumbled into the street, veering toward the kid, legs churning. Clumsily, he dipped and grabbed. And this time he held on. He kept going, half-carrying, half-sliding the boy toward the other side. With a final lunge, Mark half-fell, half-dove, taking the kid with him to the pavement. They landed side by side and skidded on the ice, piling up against the far curb. The van slid past them and through the intersection, tail first.

Finally Josh felt the muscles in his legs come

to life. He moved, Skye moved with him. The other little kids—a girl and boy, Josh saw—stood where they were, confusion in their eyes. Josh heard a door slam shut. A woman hurried toward them, high heels clicking, from down the street where her van had come to rest. She helped the small boy stand, touching him, examining his face, his head. Josh and Skye eased Mark to his feet. He walked unsteadily back to the other kids and stood with them.

"Are you okay?" the woman asked the little boy. "Do you hurt anywhere? Can you walk?" Her face was pale, her hands were shaking. The kid nodded his head, then shook it, then nodded it again.

Mark shuffled across the street, hand in hand with the boy and girl, blue eyes focused over the woman's shoulder. "You barely missed him," he said. "You should drive slower. He is someone's precious child."

"Yes," she answered. "Are you all right?" She kept her eyes on Mark as she walked the little boy to the sidewalk.

"Scared," Mark said. He put his hand on his chest. "Heart thumping."

"But you're okay otherwise?"

Mark nodded, but Josh didn't buy it. Mark and the woman both looked as if they'd been run over. Josh felt wiped out himself.

The woman eyed the little boy once more, up and down. "I need to call your parents, honey. Do you know your phone number?"

The boy nodded, but he didn't—or couldn't—say anything. Luckily, the little girl knew the number and gave it and the boy's name to the woman, who used her cell phone to call the boy's mom. Now the woman kept her voice calm.

She finished her call and knelt in front of the boy, looking him in the face. She straightened his hat and thumbed away a smear of dirt from his cheek. "Your mom will be here in a minute," she said, wiping at her eye. "Then we'll get you and your little friends to school."

"Okay," he whispered.

She stood and looked at Mark, who gazed toward her car, then up at the sky. "You big kids should go ahead to school," she said. "We'll be okay here." She kept looking at Mark. "But I don't know what would have happened if..." Her voice faded.

Josh wanted to tell her what would have happened if Mark hadn't done what he'd done, but he thought she already knew.

"Thank you," she said to Mark.

He shrugged, as if he did this kind of thing

every day. "We're late," he said to no one in particular, and started down the sidewalk. He planted one foot in front of the other, like a baby just learning to walk. Josh fell in step next to him, afraid he might have to catch him if he collapsed. Skye bookended him on his other side.

"My dad says those who don't act are no better off than those who can't," Mark said.

"I froze," Josh said.

"So did I," Skye said. "I *thought* about what I should do."

"My dad says I should pay attention to other people," Mark said. "I'm trying."

"Are you sure you're okay?" Skye said. "You almost got killed."

Mark stopped. He took a deep breath. He tugged his hood back up. "I DON'T LIKE SPEEDING CARS ON ICE." His fingers tightened around his umbrella.

"No," Skye said.

"But you did great," Josh said.

"You turned the bad into something good," Skye said. "For the little guy. The woman." She brushed some half-frozen, mashed-up leaves from the yellow of Mark's chest. The shoulder and sleeve of his jacket were scuffed and dirty. "Let's get you to school," she said, "so you can sit down."

"Superheroes don't need to sit down," Josh said. "They're never tired, they're always ready for the next thing."

Mark didn't look at Josh, but he smiled. He held his head a little higher.

They walked mostly in silence the rest of the way. Josh was busy with his thoughts. Why hadn't *he* done anything? What was wrong with him? How would he react if something like that ever happened again?

Finally they got to school. Mark went ahead to wash out the scrapes on his hands and maybe go to the nurse.

"Hey, Joshster!" Corey was waiting by the entrance with Bunk and Alex. "Got those skates yet, Josh buddy?" Corey breathed out a chestful of white air. "I know that hole in the pond is icing over."

"I'm working on it."

"It won't take long in this weather. Ice thick enough to drive on."

"It's cool," Alex said. "You gotta be there when the ice is new and smooth."

Corey gave Alex a look, and Alex shut up.

"Hey, Skye, playing soccer today?" Bunk said.

"The field's frozen." She tried to walk around

Corey, but he blocked her way.

"Is little Skye afraid she'll fall down and go boom?" Corey said. He laughed, Bunk laughed, Alex giggled.

Skye pushed past Corey, but he snuck out his foot and she tripped, losing her balance and sprawling on the sidewalk.

"You should watch your step, Skye," Corey said. He and his buddies hurried past her and into the building.

Josh stared after them, not breathing. There was still time to say something before the doors swung shut: *Hey!* or *Stop!* or *Loser!* Anything. But the words stuck in his throat. The doors closed. He stood there. Frozen again.

Skye sat up, sputtering. He helped her to her feet, fighting off a sick feeling in his stomach. Her face was red, a clump of snow stuck to the frame of her glasses, one of her gloves was torn.

He should have said something, he should have done something. What was he afraid of? What was the worst thing that could have happened? Having Corey plant him face-down in the snow next to Skye? Not so bad. And not the reason he wimped out, really. He knew the truth—Corey ruled, and Josh wanted to stay on his good side.

"Will you go with me?" she said.

"Where?" Josh asked, but he already knew where.

"Mrs. Drager. I can't take him anymore."

"Sure," he said, his throat lumping up. What else could he say? "When?"

"Now."

They pushed through the office door, Skye in the lead, and stood at the counter in front of Mrs. Benedict's desk, waiting for her to look up. At last her face broke into a smile.

"Mr. Showalter," she said. "How you doin'?"

"Good," Josh said. "But we have to see Mrs. Drager."

"We?" She eyed Skye. "You and this young lady, you mean?"

"Skye," she said.

"Aren't you supposed to be on your way to the classroom by now?" To prove her point, Mrs. Benedict stared up at the clock while its second hand inched past the numbers.

"We're here to see Mrs. Drager." Skye pulled off her torn glove and dangled it over the counter.

"What's that?" Mrs. Benedict said.

"My new glove, ruined," Skye said. "Corey Kitchens tripped me on purpose. He's been picking on me and other kids all year."

"Corey? Student Council President Corey?

He's from a very fine family. I'm sure it was an accident."

"You don't know Corey. We want to see Mrs. Drager."

"Off limits," Mrs. Benedict said.

"What?" Skye's voice broke a little.

"I am the moat." Mrs. Benedict frowned. "Mrs. Drager's office is the castle. Off limits. This is her busiest time of the day—announcements, meetings, conferences, phone calls."

"We'll wait."

"You'll be tardy without an excuse. Navigating the moat in a leaky canoe, without a paddle."

"Can't we just see her for a minute?" Josh said. Mrs. Drager's door was mostly closed, but her light was on, and he could hear talking. Maybe he should just yell at her. He could bypass Mrs. Benedict and her watchdog attitude. But that wouldn't be a good way to meet the principal. Especially if Mrs. Benedict was following orders. "Corey can be nice—he's nice to me—but he really is picking on Skye and Mark Silverthorn."

Mrs. Benedict pointed to a "Dynamic Dozen" poster on the office wall, a list of ways to deal with bullies: show a strong posture; display a powerful attitude; keep up your self-esteem;

maintain friendships; use "I-messages" to let the bully know how you feel; don't let the bully see that he/she has gotten the better of you; don't take the bullying personally; learn self-defense for confidence; try acting like a friend instead of an enemy; walk away; stay away; tell an adult.

"If you think you're having a problem with Corey Kitchens, you need to follow those suggestions," Mrs. Benedict said, "and follow them in order. 'Tell an adult' is last."

"I've tried most of those," Skye said. "They didn't work. Not with Corey."

"*Most* isn't all." Her smile was gone. "Mrs. Drager can't see you today."

Skye stared at her for a moment, then shrugged. "Have a nice week," she said. "Let's go, Josh."

They hurried out the door; they were going to be late. Josh felt sorry for Skye, not so sorry for himself. He was still on Corey's good side. "'Have a nice week'?" he said.

Skye smiled grimly. "I was trying to act like a friend instead of an enemy."

❋ 10 ❋
The FBI Arrives

Alex rushed into the classroom just as the bell was ringing. He announced to Ms. Murphy that Mark would be late. The nurse was calling Mark's parents to take him to the doctor to get checked out.

Just as Josh and Skye pushed through the school doors for lunch recess, a big black car pulled up and parked in a visitor's parking space. Mark and his dad got out. Corey, Bunk, and Alex, moving toward the soccer field, stopped and stared.

Mark's dad did look a little out of place. He wore a dark blue suit and white shirt and an olive-and-blue flowery tie.

Josh was relieved to see Mark looked like

his old self. Josh and Skye waited for him while he went inside with his dad to check in at the office.

"Was that his old man?" Corey said.

"His dad," Skye said.

"What's he do?" Bunk said.

"He helps people," Josh said.

"What's that mean?" Corey said.

"It means he helps people," Skye said.

"So he's a doctor or lawyer or something?" Bunk said.

"Or a cop?" Corey said. "Like a government cop? My dad says government cops—the FBI and the rest of 'em—wear suits and drive big plain-looking cars."

The school door opened. Mark and his dad came out. His dad had his arm around Mark's shoulders. "Why don't you ask him?" Skye said in a loud voice. "Ask him what he does."

Mark and his dad stopped. Corey studied the ground. "It's Josh and Skye," Mark's dad said. "Good seeing you again."

"You, too," Skye said.

"Hi." Josh studied Mr. Silverthorn's face. It could be a cop face. Or maybe he was on the other side of the law. Maybe he'd moved his family here to get *away* from the FBI. Didn't Mafia guys always wear suits and drive big black cars?

"Mark did a brave thing today," Skye said.

"Oh?" Mark's dad said. "Mark told me it wasn't a big thing. He said the car was a long way off when he pushed the boy out of the way."

"It was a ways off," Josh said, trying to keep Mark out of hot water. "But not *that* far." He also wanted Mark's dad to understand what Mark had risked.

Mr. Silverthorn gazed at Mark, a worried, admiring expression on his face. He looked as if he wanted to say something, but then he didn't. He gave Mark a big hug and held on. Mark just stood there, stiff and embarrassed. "You're a gift, Marky," his dad murmured finally. He let go and headed toward the parking lot. "Be careful."

Mark studied the ground.

"Come and see us again, you two," Mr. Silverthorn called back.

"We will," Skye said.

Josh just smiled. A little. What would Corey think of him being out at Mark's house?

They watched Mark's dad get in his car and drive off. Without him there, with the excitement gone, Corey seemed to stand taller. "What's your old man do for a job, hero? Or do we call you *Marky*?"

Mark didn't answer. He was taking his

camera out of his pack. He aimed it at the soccer field, where kids were warming up, dribbling and juggling balls.

"Did you hear me, Sillycorn?" Corey said.

Mark nodded, but kept his eye on the viewfinder, his mouth closed.

"What's he do?"

"He helps families," Mark said without looking at Corey.

"Geek," Corey said. "But we have to feel sorry for you, I guess." He looked at Josh. "Right, Joshster?"

"Right," Josh said, trying to sound half-sincere, half-sarcastic, trying to please everyone. Was that possible?

Corey started away from the school building, and Bunk and Alex followed. Corey looked up at the gray sky. "Winter's definitely here," he said. "Think snow, Joshster. And ice. And skates."

When he got home, Josh looked up the FBI on the Internet to see if he could find out anything, to see if it was really possible that Mark's dad was an FBI agent. There was lots of stuff, but nothing that would help him decide, based on what Mark's dad dressed like and what kind of car he drove, that he worked for the FBI. Or didn't.

Josh waited until after dinner, until Lindsay and her curiosity were in bed, and then called Skye. They hadn't had a chance to talk, and he wanted to see if she was still holding up. "You doing okay?" he said.

"Thinking about making a Corey voodoo doll out of my torn glove."

"Those things only work in movies," Josh said. "Maybe you should talk to your dad instead."

"'Tell an adult' is last on the list—remember?"

"He's not just any adult," Josh said. "He's your dad."

"I know," she said. "So I'm saving him until only a dad will do. I'm not there yet. Besides, he's got his hands full with a big story for the paper. But thanks—thanks for calling."

That night Josh was visited by a parade of disturbing dreams featuring Mark and Skye, Corey and Bunk, and Alex. But his last dream was populated by strangers, panicked and running. A huge cloud of spaceships shaped and patterned like soccer balls flew silently over the summit of Rathdrum Mountain and descended on the town. From corkscrew tubes on the ships' undersides, giant streams of frigid vapor erupted, freezing the ground, coating houses with thick layers of ice, turning the pine forests white, paralyzing everything that moved. Josh tried to run, but the air shimmered with cold, turning his blood to syrup. His legs wouldn't work. He couldn't even scream.

He forced his eyes open, his heart pounding. His blankets lay in a heap on the floor. Shivering, exhausted, he tried to untangle dreams from what seemed like dreams. Dim light filtered in through his window. It was Tuesday morning. He got out of bed and checked the thermometer: fourteen degrees. The spaceships had done their work.

❄ **11** ❄
Surprise Package

J osh's mom offered to give him a ride to school, but he would put up with the cold; he wanted to walk with Mark and Skye. When he opened the front door to look for them, he saw a red plastic bag sitting on the steps. *Roper's Sporting Goods* was printed on it, and underneath the printing someone had scrawled another name: Josh.

He stared at it until his mom yelled at him to close the door before they all froze. He picked up the bag. It was heavy, and he began to have a dancing feeling in his chest. Lindsay, then his mom, came into the living room as he set the bag in the middle of the floor.

"What is it?" his mom said. Lindsay tried

to peek inside the bag, but Josh pulled it away from her.

"I don't know," he said. "It was on the front steps. It has my name on it."

"Open it, Joshy," Lindsay said.

His mom nodded.

Josh opened the bag. He pulled out some white tissue paper, then a box.

He couldn't believe it. Hockey skates, the box said. Size nine—his size. He pulled off the lid, and there they were: black, glossy leather; shiny, silvery blades. He looked up at his mom, but her expression told him she didn't have a clue. Which meant his dad wouldn't know anything, either; Mom controlled the checkbook. Josh searched through the bag, through the box, for some kind of note or card. Nothing.

So not his dad, not his mom. Mark and Skye didn't care about ice skating, and they didn't want him hanging around Corey and Bunk. Alex? Josh didn't think so. He didn't think Alex would buy skates for someone he barely knew. Which brought him to Corey, who liked Josh, who seemed interested in getting him out to the pond.

Josh's mom looked through the bag. "Who?"

Josh shook his head. "I don't know."

"One of your friends?"

"Maybe."

"Who would know your size?"

"I don't know." But Corey could have figured it out pretty close. He'd seen Josh's footprint in the snow at the pond, right next to his own.

"I think you need to find out, Josh. These are expensive. We need to find out if the parents know about this."

"I'll try." But he wasn't sure how hard he would try. He had skates now. He didn't want to think about giving them back.

❄ ❄ ❄

Josh debated with himself about whether to tell Skye and Mark about the skates. But not for long—how could he keep the news to himself? When they showed up, he told them. They agreed with Josh: it had to be Corey.

"He's really trying to get in good with your dad," Skye said.

"My dad's not going to be fooled by a kid."

"Corey doesn't know that," Skye said. "You should have a lot of cool toys by the time he gets to high school."

"Maybe he just wants me to play hockey with him. Maybe he just likes me."

"Corey likes himself," Skye said. "He keeps

Bunk around to laugh at his jokes and do some of his dirty work."

"I think they've changed," Josh said.

"Those two will never change," Mark said. "They're colder than ice."

Josh was tired of arguing. "We'll see, I guess," was all he said.

Corey, Bunk, and Alex were standing around by the school entrance.

"The Joshster and friends," Corey said.

"I got some skates," Josh said.

"Really?" Corey said. "Awesome."

Josh studied his face, looking for some kind of sign. But he couldn't see anything behind the smile.

"You got skates?" Alex said. "You got *skates*?" He seemed more excited about it than anyone. He smiled big, teetering back and forth on his shoes like a plastic punch-me bag. "Where'd ya get 'em?"

"Somebody left them on his doorstep," Skye said.

"Was it you, Corey?" Josh said. "My mom wants me to find out."

"Wishes—sometimes they come true," Corey said.

"Now you can come out the first day," Bunk said. "I've got a stick you can use."

"Thanks," Josh said.

"You'll love it, Josh buddy," Corey said. "You'll *love* it." He turned to Skye and Mark. "Your friends probably wouldn't like it out there, though."

"Don't worry," Skye said. "I don't do hockey."

"I will be occupied elsewhere," Mark said.

"Whatever," Corey said.

"How soon will the ice be ready?" Josh said.

"We went by the pond this morning," Corey said. "It's getting close. I'm thinking Thursday."

The bell rang, loud.

Ms. Murphy started off the day. "A week or two from now, if the cold weather continues, we might not have to worry," she said. "But so far we haven't had enough cold to put a safe layer of ice on our ponds and lakes. It's still too thin for skating or even walking on. So you need to be very careful. You know the story of Poor Rooney's Pond."

Suddenly, in the warm classroom, Josh felt a chill. Skye raised her hand. "We—Josh and Mark and me—don't know it," she said.

Ms. Murphy nodded. "Sorry, Skye. I guess I forgot about those of you who recently moved here."

Across the room, a kid waved his hand in

the air.

"Yes, Miguel?"

"I heard that the Poor Rooney story isn't true."

"Who told you that?"

"A friend."

"You and your friend should visit the library, Miguel. The librarian can show you newspaper articles."

"It's true?" Miguel said.

"My mother went to school with Jimmy Rooney forty years ago," Ms. Murphy said. "She saw him at school one day in early December. He and some friends decided to go to the pond in the afternoon. They wanted to be the first ones to skate there that winter. My mother never saw him again. His friends watched him go through the ice. They couldn't save him."

Why didn't Corey know about Jimmy Rooney? Now Josh wasn't sure he wanted to go to Poor Rooney's Pond on that first day, at least not to skate. Maybe he'd just watch.

He felt Skye's eyes on him. "Don't let him talk you into going out on the ice," she whispered.

"I'll go when it's safe," Josh said.

Mark just stared at the table.

✽ ✽ ✽

"Do you want to come out to my house this afternoon?" Mark asked Josh and Skye on the way home. "I want to show you something."

They checked with their parents and got the okay.

Despite the weather, Mark kept his camera busy. He stopped to take pictures of cattle, sheep, horses, the llamas, luring them all close with little carrots he'd stashed in his pack. The black-and-white bobtailed dog came out to greet them again. It sat at the fence, posing, then herded a couple of stray sheep back to where they belonged while Mark clicked away.

When they got to his driveway, they stopped again while Mark snapped pictures of his fields and house. Finally they went inside. Josh was hoping for some hot chocolate.

Instead, they said hello to Mark's mom, working at a desk in a book-filled den, and went upstairs to the land of flimsy floors. Mark's room looked the same: undisturbed by human kid. Josh sat on the corner of Mark's bed, but Mark looked a little nervous. So Josh found a chair next to Skye. They took off their coats and watched while Mark hooked up a cable between his camera and computer.

"Wait there," he said. From a distance they

watched as he downloaded pictures from his camera and they appeared on the screen. He sat down, blocking the display, and began playing with the mouse, the keys, concentrating.

"What are you doing, Mark?" Skye said after several minutes.

"Creating," Mark said. "Photographs—poems without words. They're taking me a little longer than I figured." He kept working.

Finally he clicked the mouse and leaned back. His printer whirred into action. It slowly spit out one sheet of paper. He picked it up and studied it while two more sheets rolled out. Then he stood and brought the two pieces of paper over to Josh and Skye, his grin wide and proud.

He handed one sheet of paper to Skye, one to Josh. They were two copies of the same photo, a full-page-size picture of Mark's property, taken from the road. The house was there, the barn, the silo, the car parked in the driveway.

But then things got weird. Out near the fence, a black-and-white dog smiled a big-toothed smile at the camera. Behind the dog, cattle grazed, horses nuzzled each other. Most of the sheep flocked together, but one sat behind the wheel of the car, ready to drive to town. Llamas stood like guards on either side of the front door. They each wore a police hat. Next to the house grew a grove of tall, leafy trees. Nibbling at their upper branches was a giraffe. Nearby, a hippopotamus wallowed in a pond, which connected to a moat, which circled the house.

Josh kept staring at the picture. He knew Mark had brought all the stuff together, but it looked real, it all fit. Not like some of the amateurish photo blending he'd seen. He had to tell himself to stay put, that there was no point in getting up and looking out the window to see if the giraffe was still nibbling, the hippo still wallowing.

"How did you do this?" Skye said without looking up from her photo.

"Do you like it?" Mark said. "Now we have everything—animals, a pond, big trees."

"It's great," Skye said. "It looks like a real farm. Kind of."

"Computer magic," Mark said.

"But some of these you didn't take," Skye said. "Not today, anyway."

"Internet," Mark said. "I could have put dinosaurs in the moat."

"Cool," Josh said, imagining the possibilities. "Can I show this to my parents?"

"They're yours," Mark said. "THE OLD

BAXTER PLACE, TRANSFORMED."

They went downstairs. Josh and Skye put their pictures in plastic bags Mark found for them. Finally, Josh got his hot chocolate. They sat at the kitchen table and drank it slowly, not talking about Corey or ice skating. When they walked outside to leave, though, Josh glanced at his photo. He looked around and thought about a real pond here, a real moat, frozen over. He pictured himself circling the house on skates, gliding over that smooth surface with the cold wind in his ears. He smiled.

❄ 12 ❄
Hitting the Ice

The cold weather continued through Tuesday and into Wednesday. That afternoon, Corey told Josh to bring his skates to school the next day for the first skate. The ice was thick enough to survive a cannonball, Corey said. On the way home, Josh tried talking Skye and Mark into going out to the pond just to watch, but they weren't interested.

Josh was going to ask his mom and dad for permission to go. He really was. But the more he thought about it, the more he realized they could say no. Parents just did that sometimes. And then what? So he told his mom, who told Mrs. Sinclair, that he'd be going to Mark's house after school on Thursday.

When he woke up Thursday morning, clouds hung low and dark. Two inches of snow had fallen during the night. The thermometer read thirteen degrees. Inside he felt like one of Mark's computer photos—eager Josh, excited Josh, nervous Josh, all mixed together. As he got out of bed, he thought again about telling his parents he'd been invited to go skating. He pictured his mom hesitating but his dad jumping in, telling Josh it was okay, just to use his head.

And he would use his head. He wouldn't step on the ice unless he decided it was as tough as that crusty, frozen dirt in his backyard.

Before he got dressed, he tried on his skates for the fourth or fifth time. They felt good over his thick socks, a perfect fit.

❄ ❄ ❄

Mark wasn't smiling his usual smile when he and Skye stopped by for Josh. His hood was up, his umbrella hung from a loop on his backpack. He searched the sky for signs of snow. "DANGEROUS WEATHER," he said as they started down the street.

"Skating weather," Josh said. The skates—hidden inside his pack—were heavy. A hungry wind chewed at his face and swirled dry snow around his feet as he thought of a boy named Rooney.

"You're really going?" Skye said.

"Yeah."

"Your parents know?"

"They think I'm going to Mark's."

"I wish you were," Mark said.

"I'll go," Skye said softly.

"To the pond?" Josh said.

She nodded. Mark's worried look grew darker. Josh watched him, hoping he'd say he'd join them. He didn't. "Be careful, Skye," was all he said.

"Why'd you change your mind?" Josh asked Skye.

"If you get in trouble, those guys won't help."

"I'm not going to get in trouble. I might not even skate."

"I'm going, anyway," Skye said.

"Thanks." Josh's backpack suddenly felt lighter.

❀ ❀ ❀

The dirt road was covered with snow, and more sifted down lightly from the thick, low-lying clouds. The day had grown darker, even though it wasn't yet four o'clock. Up ahead of Josh and Skye, Corey and Bunk led the group through the trees. In between marched the three other guys from Corey's photo, then Alex, alone. He kept looking back, as if to make sure Josh and Skye hadn't disappeared.

They walked into the clearing, and for a moment Josh thought he was in a different place. The pond, a smooth sheet of solid white now, blended in with the snow-covered ground surrounding it. On the opposite bank, the pines were transformed by a glittery frosting. The scene looked like the photo. All it needed were some kids out in the middle. The wind kicked up a bit, and Josh pulled his stocking cap lower over his ears.

Something buzz-cracked behind him and he glanced back, catching a fleeting glimpse of movement through the trees. But then there was nothing. An animal, maybe. A bird. A falling seed cone, frozen brittle. He breathed in the smell of snow and pine.

Corey, the other seventh-graders, and Alex walked to the edge of the pond and leaned their hockey sticks against a low, scrubby tree. Bunk had brought an extra stick for Josh.

"Your feet must be itching for those skates, huh, Josh buddy?" Corey said.

Josh squeezed out a weak laugh. His feet felt comfortable right where they were—in his shoes. He wondered what the ice looked like under that thin layer of snow.

Corey slipped Skye a dirty look. "Why aren't you hanging out with your little geek friend, Sillycorn?" he said, picking up a soft-ball-size rock. She frowned and shook her head disgustedly, and he shot-putted the rock onto the ice, maybe twenty feet from shore. It clattered across the surface, kicking up puffs of snow. "Solid," he said.

"Looks good," Josh said. But he wasn't convinced. He weighed as much as fifty of those rocks.

"Why don't you get 'em on?" Corey said to Josh. One of the seventh-graders, a guy named Eli, began moving away, walking the thick ice along the shoreline, his skates slung over his shoulder. The other two older guys, Drew and Lee, sat down on a log and got their skates out of their bags. Alex stood near them, shifting from foot to foot.

Josh stared out at the ice, at Eli circling toward the other side of the pond. "I think I might wait a while."

Corey laughed. Bunk laughed. Alex forced a giggle. Drew and Lee looked up but kept working on their skates. "Wait for what, Joshster?" Corey said. "It's going to be dark in an hour."

Josh couldn't think of anything to say. He didn't want to admit that the ice scared him.

"He wants to wait," Skye said.

"Who asked you?" Bunk said.

Skye glared at him.

"C'mon, Josh buddy," Corey said. "You wouldn't want to waste those new skates, would you?"

"I'm not sure about the ice," Josh confessed. "That kid—Jimmy Rooney—died here."

Corey belched out a laugh. "You don't believe that, do you?"

"It's true," Skye said. "Ms. Murphy told us."

"Shut up, four eyes!" Corey said.

Josh looked at Skye and got a sick feeling in his stomach. "I'll just wait. I'll watch you guys for a while and see how it goes."

"Sure," Corey said. "You're a good guy. I like you."

"Your dad's the big-time coach," Bunk said. Corey shot him a look.

"I'm not going to force you to go out there, Josh buddy," Corey said.

Josh let out a sigh. For a minute he'd thought Corey wasn't going to take no for an answer.

"Besides, every good plan has a backup." Corey walked over to Alex and stopped a foot away, taller and broad-shouldered and spring-loaded. His eyes were ice. He leaned his face closer. "You're the backup, *fat boy*."

Backup? Plan? Josh's stomach lurched again.

"Get on your skates, Alex," Corey said.

Alex plopped down on the log next to Drew and Lee. "No," he whined, but he began untying his shoes as if his fingers were enchanted.

"You thought you were safe, didn't you, Alex buddy," Corey said. "You thought you'd found a bigger, fatter sucker. And you were glad to find him, weren't you."

Staring at his shoes, Alex shook his head.

"C'mon, wide buddy," Corey said. "Don't be shy. Tell Josh the plan."

Alex raised his head and looked at Josh. "A tester," he said softly. "You were going to test the ice."

Josh felt his knees weaken. He was inside that nightmare where he was being frozen, where he wanted to run but couldn't.

"That's what Alex buddy thought, anyway," Corey said. "He was eager to come out and watch. He even spent his hard-earned money on those new skates of yours. But he always was my first choice."

"You lied to me," Alex said to Corey. But his fingers kept moving. He had one shoe off, one skate on.

"Doesn't matter, blimp boy. 'Cause you're not such a good guy. 'Cause I don't like you much."

Skye was standing by Josh now. "You're crazy, Corey," she said.

Corey ignored her. "So you're going to be our test pilot, Porky. You're going out and skating around that pond until you've tested every inch of it." He leaned down and grabbed Alex's coat collar and twisted. "Or I'll hurt you. Bad."

Josh couldn't believe he'd been so stupid. Alex had bought the skates. Everything nice Corey had said was just an act to get Josh out here. And the only reason Corey wasn't forcing Josh onto the ice now was because his dad was the basketball coach.

Skye and Mark had been right.

He felt sick for Alex and relieved for himself and disgusted that he could feel relieved. If he volunteered to go, would Corey still make Alex go, too? Josh looked at the pond. He imagined a paper-thin sheet of ice beneath the white frosting. He couldn't say the words. He couldn't go out there.

Alex had his skates on now. "Couldn't we just wait a few more days?" Josh managed to say.

"We could," Corey said, "but why should we? I'm ready. We have our guinea pig, and I do mean pig, right here." He grabbed the shoulders of Alex's coat and pulled him to his feet.

"Get your hands off him," Skye said, and tried to wedge Corey away. But Bunk gave her a push, and she slipped and pancaked onto the ground. Her glasses flipped into the snow. When she put them back on, a smear of white hid one of her eyes. Josh helped her back to her feet. Why did she always have to stick her neck out? He could feel her fingers trembling through her gloves.

Corey pushed hard and Alex tumbled backward. He landed on his rear. Snow mushroomed up. He grunted. He sat there for a second, looking dazed, then rolled to his knees and finally stood, half-facing the pond. His legs wobbled, maybe from trying to balance on his blades, maybe from fear. Or indecision: *The pond? Or Corey?* "It's okay," he said. "I'll do it."

"What?" Skye's voice was shaky.

"I'll do it. The ice looks safe." He faked a smile.

Safe? Josh thought. That's what poor Jimmy

Rooney believed. But at least Alex would have a chance on the ice. It was better than Corey beating him up and then making him go, anyway.

Alex took one unsteady step toward the ice, then another. Josh blinked at the cold. It—or something—was bringing tears to his eyes.

"Don't do it," Skye said to Alex. "Let him beat you up. Make him try to drag you."

Alex took another step, wordless, as if he were in a trance.

"It's better to get beat up than die, Alex," she said. "You could die out there."

"Shut up, freak," Corey said. "Alex buddy knows it's safe. Even for a whale."

"If it's so safe, why don't *you* go?" she said.

"Because I don't *have* to go. Not when blimp boy will go for me."

"Don't do it," Skye said again, but Alex stepped out, both feet.

"Good boy," Corey said. "Ready for your instructions?"

Alex nodded.

"You sure you should be doing this, Corey?" Drew said.

Corey just stared at him, long and cold, and Drew looked away, then down at his skates.

"Your job is to go out there and test that ice,"

Corey said. "Nice and slow, covering all of it, but especially the big center section that freezes over last. If anything looks or feels funny, you're gonna tell me. Okay?"

Alex nodded again.

A small, dark bird landed on the ice ten feet from shore and hopped three times, leaving tiny tracks in the snow. Josh remembered Mark telling him about coal miners taking canaries into the mines with them. Alex was like one of those canaries, traveling down that long dark shaft, with no way to get out.

It could have been me, Josh thought. Maybe it should have been. But he couldn't make himself take Alex's place. He shuffled to the low-growing tree and picked up Alex's hockey stick. "For balance," he said, reaching it out to Alex. But it wasn't for balance. It was something to hold onto in case the ice opened up and swallowed him.

Alex took the stick. "Thanks."

Josh nodded. But what had he done, really? His opportunities to be brave kept on coming, and he kept turning away. How many more would he get?

Skye stepped onto the ice and grabbed Alex's arm, but Bunk pulled her away. "Don't mess with the plan," he growled.

"And just in case you get any ideas about heading for the other side and taking off," Corey said to Alex, "we've got our friend Eli over there to stop you." Corey waved, and across the pond, through the thickening snowflakes and deepening murk, Eli waved back. "You can try to stumble away between here and there," Corey continued, "but we'll catch you. And make you sorry you tried."

Alex pushed off and headed counterclockwise along the shoreline, wobbly-legged, holding the stick across his body like a guy on a high wire. Drew and Lee stood, skates on, eyeing his progress. Corey and Bunk sat on the log and began untying their shoes, but their attention was on the ice.

Alex reached the other side, still hugging the shoreline. But Eli shouted something at him and he moved out a little as he continued his circle. Skye edged out farther on the ice.

Josh took a deep breath and followed her.

"All day," Corey said behind them. Disgust dripped from his words. "We're going to be here all day at this rate."

Josh looked over his shoulder. Corey and Bunk were searching the ground, kicking at it with the blades of their skates. They uncovered and unearthed some rocks, golf-ball-size, and picked them up. They tottered toward the ice with two or three rocks in each hand.

"What are you doing?" Skye said.

"Blimp boy's not doing us any good," Corey said. "We already know the ice along the shore's okay."

"We're gonna give him a reason to explore the middle," Bunk said.

They stood next to Josh and Skye and waited for Alex to get closer.

Skye grabbed Josh's arm. Her grip tightened as Alex got within a hundred feet, then fifty, barely ten feet from shore.

What about getting help from somewhere? Josh wondered. Without skates, he and Skye could try to make a run for it. But how long would that take? And what would happen to Alex in the meantime?

Bunk heaved a rock. It clattered at Alex's feet. He looked up, surprise tugging at his face, and nearly fell. "Get out!" Corey shouted at him and threw another rock. It glanced off his skate and rattled across the ice. "Get out to the middle, you tub of guts, or we'll start aiming at you!"

Alex came to a stop twenty-five feet away. His face was red and grim, his eyes squinted against the snow. Bunk rifled another rock. It whizzed past Alex's head. Holding the hockey stick across his chest, he started away from shore.

"Closer to the middle!" Corey shouted at Alex's back. He tossed a rock that skipped past Alex's skates, kicking up puffs of snow.

Josh couldn't stop watching what was happening, but he sensed Skye's eyes on him. Why couldn't he do something? *Why couldn't he?*

Suddenly a rock—a big one—came out of nowhere and landed right next to Corey's skates. Josh felt the ice under his feet vibrate. "ALEX MOVES OUT TOWARD THE DANGEROUS PART OF THE ICE," a voice announced. Turning, Josh saw Mark, dressed warm in his hooded yellow coat, pack on his back, striped umbrella in the crook of his arm, camera in his hand, standing on a snowy knoll in a little clearing, just beyond where Drew and Lee were standing, their mouths open. "COREY AND BUNK, TOO COWARDLY TO GO THEMSELVES, FORCE ALEX TO TEST THE ICE."

Corey and Bunk turned. The surprise on their faces evaporated, replaced by hate. "Shut up, you little creep!" Corey shouted. "You better get out of here before I kill you!"

"DON'T GO ANY FARTHER, ALEX. THE COWARDS CAN'T MAKE YOU."

Alex stopped. Not yet to the middle, he turned to look back.

"Get the geek, Drew." Corey said.

Drew didn't move. He pointed to his skates.

"Take 'em off," Corey said.

"I don't think so," Drew said.

"Lee?" Corey said. Lee stayed where he was. His skates stayed on.

"COREY TRIES TO GIVE ORDERS BUT NO ONE LISTENS," Mark said.

Corey said something under his breath. He started for shore with Bunk at his shoulder. Glide, glide, glide. Thump. They reached the bank.

"COREY AND BUNK STOP THROWING ROCKS. ALEX HAS A CHANCE TO ESCAPE. GO, ALEX, GO."

Josh looked at Alex. He was frozen in place. Where could he go, anyway? Eli, still in his shoes, could easily get him. Once Alex got to land, his skates would be nearly worthless. Which was what Corey and Bunk were discovering right now as they wobbled toward Mark.

"COREY AND BUNK PROVE ONCE AND FOR ALL THAT THEIR MOUTHS ARE BIGGER THAN THEIR BRAINS," Mark said. "THEY ATTEMPT TO SKATE ON DIRT."

It was slow going for them, but they closed the distance between themselves and Mark, who was holding his position. He raised his camera and snapped off shots of Corey and Bunk, struggling toward him, then aimed it out toward the pond and Alex, still in the same spot.

"GO, ALEX," Mark said as Corey and Bunk got closer. "THE DIRT SKATERS ARE DISTRACTED. BUT THEY'RE GETTING TOO CLOSE. MARK WILL HAVE TO LEAVE. HE WILL GO GET HELP. THE BULLIES WILL BE IN TROUBLE UNTIL THEIR BEARDS TURN GRAY." He aimed his camera one more time as Corey and Bunk got within a few feet. "SMILE," he said, and bolted away, kicking up small rooster-tails of snow, leaving Corey and Bunk clenching their fists and breathing hard.

"You can't run forever, Sillycorn!" Corey shouted after him. "We'll find you!"

"I'LL BE BACK," Mark answered. All Josh could see now was his yellow jacket, flitting through the trees like a giant canary. "WITH BIG PEOPLE."

Corey and Bunk turned to the pond. "Liar," Corey spit. "He's not coming back."

"Who'd listen to him, anyway?" Bunk said.

"He'd have to find someone as crazy as he

is," Corey said. He and Bunk high-fived as they hobbled down the bank and onto the ice.

"We're going," Drew said.

"Why?" Corey said. "You think he's really going to tell someone?"

"Hard to know with that kid," Lee said. He sat down on the log and began unlacing his skates. Drew joined him.

"Quitters," Corey said, but Drew and Lee didn't even look up.

"He's not a liar," Josh said. He had to try to convince Corey and Bunk that Mark meant to come back.

"Or crazy," Skye said.

"Shut up, Skye," Corey said. "If you weren't so skinny and useless, I'd make you join your fat friend out there."

"Get moving, elephant boy!" Bunk shouted at Alex.

"Or it'll be snowing rocks on you!" Corey said. He cocked his arm and chucked one straight at Alex, who had to dance awkwardly out of the way. He began moving again, cautious, eyes on the ice at his feet.

"We're outta here." Drew slung his skates over his shoulder and started toward the path.

"You're the crazy one, Corey," Lee said. He followed Drew into the gloom. Josh wasn't comforted by their leaving. They weren't exactly on the side of the good guys, but at least they seemed reasonable, maybe able to put a lid on Corey's sick scheme, or be there if something went wrong.

"Chickens," Corey called after them. He began clucking and chicken-winging his arms. Bunk was the only one who laughed.

Out on the ice, Alex moved closer to the center but veered off before he got there and went into a ragged orbit. He crossed and criss-crossed the wide expanse of white that framed the newly-frozen middle. With his hockey stick at right angles to his body and the dusting of snow covering his clothes, he looked like a snowman come to life, testing his new-found abilities. His movements were robotic, stiffened by cold and caution.

Bunk took a step and threw a rock. It hit the ice and bounced into Alex's leg. "The middle!" Bunk screamed. "Or you'll be out there all night."

Corey snickered. Alex leaned over and rubbed his lower leg. He wiped at his eyes, then skated silently on, crossing near the center. From the other side Eli launched another rock, and Alex took a U-turn, heading straight for the middle.

"You're lookin' better, lard guts!" Corey called out, but he threw another rock, anyway.

Alex looked up as it bounced in front of him. He seemed to lose his balance, wobbling, paddling the hockey stick through the air. Then his right skate caught, spinning him sideways. And down.

Shoulder first, he slammed into the ice. A loud crack boomed across the pond. A wall of green-white water geysered up around him. He disappeared. His hockey stick pogoed into the air and rattled to the frozen surface.

❄ 13 ❄
Deep Trouble

Alex's head bobbed to the surface in the middle of a dark patch of water. He'd lost his hat. His hair streamed. "Help!" he wailed. "Help me!"

"Let's go." Corey's words, secretive and urgent, came from behind Josh.

Josh turned to see Corey and Bunk heading up the bank toward their shoes. "What are you doing?" Skye said. "We have to get Alex out!"

"You have to get him out," Corey said. "I hear my mommy calling me." He was trying to be funny, but his voice quavered.

Bunk laughed nervously. "He's got his fat to keep him warm."

"Help him!" Skye shouted. "He's gonna

drown!" She started for Alex. Across the pond, Eli hurried into the trees.

"Wait," Josh said, but she didn't wait. She continued on, not looking back.

Josh spun toward shore.

"Good thinking, Josh buddy," Corey said. "We'll catch up to you and Eli on the trail." He and Bunk sat on the log, trading skates for shoes.

But Josh wasn't about to run away. He wasn't about to stand frozen in place, either. He'd had enough of doing nothing. He'd had enough of thinking of himself as less than nothing.

He hunted frantically along the shoreline for a big branch, and found one. He grabbed it with both hands. It shed its icing of snow. The limb was thick, four or five inches at the big end and six or seven feet long. But it was pretty light. He wondered how strong it was. No time to wonder. He turned and charged.

Skye was already halfway to Alex. He was still afloat. For how long? Out of the corner of his eye, Josh saw Corey and Bunk scramble to their feet and head off.

The ice was scary—solid at the shoreline, but not where Josh was going. He half-slid toward the hole, trying to keep his feet spread at the same time.

Ahead of him Skye slowed, head down, concentrating, inspecting, getting closer to Alex and the open water.

Alex had grabbed onto the ice. Pressing his gloved hands to its surface, he kicked and pulled and pushed and boosted his shoulders a foot above the water. Again the ice gave way. He went down and under, then came back up, sputtering and red-faced. Ice chunks bobbed all around him.

"Careful, Alex!" Josh called. Skye looked back. She seemed surprised to see him. Had she really thought he'd just leave? Well, why not? Why would she waste her hopes on a coward?

He called to her. "There's too much weight with both of us. I'll come from the other side to keep a little distance from you."

When they got closer to Alex, they went gently down on their hands and knees. They inched along, testing the ice as they went. Josh listened for noise, feeling for mushy give under his shaking hands.

"I need to get the hockey stick first," Skye said.

The stick was lying near the edge of the hole. "Careful," Josh repeated, trying to spread his weight over his hands and knees.

Skye bellied toward the hockey stick. "Get lower," she told him. "Your weight's more spread out that way."

Josh flattened himself on the ice. He felt like a slug—a frozen one. But slithering made sense. And he was almost there now. He dragged the branch along. The cold stabbed through his gloves and pants. He tried not to think of what was just below it.

"Help me," Alex said weakly. From ten feet away, Josh could see his lips, blue with cold, his jaw trembling.

"We're going to," Skye said. "I've got the hockey stick, Josh has a branch." Nearly spread-eagle, she thrust the stick toward Alex, who lifted a hand slowly and stiffly and grabbed. Skye held on as he closed on the stick with his other hand. She tried crab-crawling back, but she couldn't budge him. The stick bent as he tried to put some weight on it.

"Grab this one, too," Josh said. He scooted closer and pushed the fat end of the branch over the edge of the ice. Alex released his left hand from the hockey stick and gripped the limb. Holding tight, Josh side-scrambled closer—but not too close—to Skye so they'd be pulling in the same direction.

Three feet apart, they rose up on their

hands and knees and readied themselves. The ice groaned under them. "One," Skye said. "Two. Pull!"

They pulled. Alex hung on. He kicked, stirring up the water. He lunged. He whimpered and cursed.

"Hang on!" Josh said. Would Alex let go and slip under?

He gave a final surge, trying to pull himself up and onto his elbows. But one elbow broke through. He fell back, still grasping the branch, just keeping his head above water.

What now?

"SAVE YOUR STRENGTH," a voice called. "HELP IS COMING. MARK IS COMING TO HELP."

Josh looked. A figure was approaching, yellow coat, hood up, crouched, zigzagging as if he was trying to dance between the snowflakes. He held the big striped umbrella over his head with one hand, a camera to his face with the other. Mark. But where were the big people?

"You didn't go back for help?" Josh said.

"No time," Mark said.

"We need help!" Alex croaked.

"I'M HERE," Mark said. And he was now. He got down on all fours, pocketing his camera, leaving his umbrella open on the ice, and twisting in the wind. He crawled the last few feet. Would his extra weight take them all under? How much could he help?

He filled the space between Josh and Skye. He studied the water, the ice around it, twisting his hands and arms into different configurations as if designing a plan.

"BACKWARDS!" he shouted.

Alex asked no questions. Maybe his brain was half-frozen by now. He pivoted around, treading water. His head dipped nearly under, then bobbed skyward.

Suddenly Josh got a glimpse of the picture in Mark's brain. Alex needed to turn over and arch his back so he'd float high. Maybe then they'd have a chance. "Slide the hockey stick under his left armpit, Skye," Josh said.

Skye scooted closer, and Alex helped her position the business end of the stick under his arm so its tip was pointed toward the clouds. He held on with his left hand.

"GOOD, ALEX," Mark said. "GOOD."

Now it was Josh's turn. He inched toward the jagged hole, easing the limb in front of him and under Alex's right arm. Alex grabbed onto its base. "Lean back now," Josh ordered. "Get your feet and legs and butt up. Be flat and stiff."

Alex's words came out like weak machine-gun

fire: "Stiff-isn't-a-problem." He leaned back. His knees, then the tips of his skate blades, surfaced. The back of his head submerged to ear-level. He was back floating.

"GOOD," Mark said.

"Let's get you out of there," Skye said.

Up on his elbows, Josh got a two-handed grip on the branch, pressing his end of it between his upper arm and ribs. Mark helped Skye with the hockey stick. "Ready," Josh said. "Set. Go."

He pulled, shifting his weight back, pressing his shoes to the ice, hoping he wouldn't slip. And Alex moved. His head moved up over the ice, then his shoulders. He stalled.

"Pull!" Skye said. They pulled.

Alex's shoulders slid up on the ice a few more inches. Water sloshed onto the surface.

All of a sudden there was another crack. The border of ice shattered and disappeared, and Alex slipped back into the water. Josh waited for him to yell, scream, say something. But he didn't. He held on, leaning back, staying rigid. Josh looked over at Skye and Mark. Her eyes were narrowed. Mark was breathing hard, staring up at the sky. Then he looked down, concentrating on the ice. He and Skye inched back and set themselves, their arms wrapped around the stick. So did Josh.

"WE WON'T GIVE UP," Mark said.

"Even if we have to tow you all the way to shore," Skye said.

But Josh wondered what if someone else—or all of them—went in? "Let's do it," was all he said.

"One," Mark said.

"Two," Skye said.

"Three," Josh said. He threw everything he had into it—hands, arms, weight, legs, toes digging for some kind of hold. And he felt movement, he saw Alex's shoulders slide up onto the ice once more.

"PULL!" Mark said, and they pulled again.

The ice shuddered under Josh as more of Alex—half his torso—came out of the water. He moved his legs in slow motion, trying to help, and Josh and Skye and Mark didn't let up on the pressure. They inched back, leaning, pulling.

Alex was up to his waist on the ice now, with his rear and legs still in the water.

"STIFF!" Mark said, and Alex tried to arch his back.

"Pull," Skye said, and they did, together.

There was a hesitation, the sound of ice cracking, but it was a small break. More of

Alex slid out. His bottom and upper legs. He mumbled something. It sounded like a prayer.

"Again," Josh said, and they tugged in unison. This time Alex slid easily on a surface slicked by water. His skate blades ticked against the edge of the hole and bounced up and suddenly he was out all the way. Free and clear. Flat on his back, he breathed out a huge cloud of vapor. He coughed.

"I'm out?" he said. His words sounded thick.

"Hold on." Mark reached for his umbrella, collapsed it, and jammed it through a belt loop. He got out his camera and snapped off a picture of Alex.

"Pull," Skye said.

They pulled. Again and again. Getting Alex away from the hole, away from the middle of the pond, away from the thin ice. They dropped the limb and hockey stick and grabbed him by the arms. He was soaked and dripping, but he managed a smile.

❄ 14 ❄
Superheroes

"THE THREE SUPERHEROES RESCUE ALEX FROM THE ICY WATERS OF POOR ROONEY'S POND!" Mark announced.

They laughed. All of them. Josh liked the sound of *superheroes*. He liked it better than *rookies*. He didn't feel like a hero, much less a superhero, but at least he wasn't a less-than-nothing coward. He was freezing and exhausted, but he took off his coat and offered it to Alex.

"Let's get him to shore first," Skye said.

"Can you stand?" Josh said.

"I don't know." Alex's whole body was shaking now. His shoulder shuddered under Josh's touch. "I'll try."

"Take off the skates," Mark ordered, unlacing Alex's right skate. Skye started on the left while Josh draped his coat over Alex's head and shoulders and made sure he stayed sitting upright. The snow fell faster, sifting down past Josh's shirt collar. He shivered. The wind knifed through his sweatshirt and shirt.

Mark peered up at the dark sky, then out at the middle of the pond. He aimed his camera toward the hole and took more pictures. Snow swirled down on him. He made a face at it, then tugged at the cord of his hood, snugging it down. He fingered his umbrella but left it in place, saving it for later, maybe.

They got Alex to his feet, shoeless, and held onto his arms. He was heavy, soaked, and limp. Ice crystals shone on his pants. He smelled of stagnant water—mud and rotted plants and dead algae. He took a step, then another, leaving puddles behind. His socks squished. They moved him off the pond, up onto the bank.

"Take off your stuff," Skye said.

Alex gave her a look.

"Not everything," she said. "But you'll freeze if you don't get changed."

They helped him off with his coat, then he peeled off his sweater and shirt and dropped them in a heap on the ground. His skin was splotchy pink and white and covered with goose bumps. Mark whipped off his coat and sweatshirt, gave the sweatshirt to Alex, and wiggled back into his coat. Alex managed to squeeze into the sweatshirt. Sausage-skin tight, but at least it wasn't wet. Over that went

Josh's coat. They sat Alex down on a log and stripped off his socks, replacing them with his cold but dry shoes. He sat, breathing hard, shivering, half-dry, half-wet.

"Thanks," he said. It came out slurred, like *Thanksh*. "You guys saved my life."

"Not yet," Josh said. "We need to get you home before you turn into a Popsicle."

They threw everything into their backpacks, got Alex to his feet again, and headed out. At first they had to help him, but then he seemed to warm up, or maybe the idea of being on land and alive and heading home inspired him. Snow still fell thickly in the near darkness, and when Josh turned back, he could barely see the inky hole in the center of Poor Rooney's Pond.

Mark took the lead, his yellow coat bright in the gloom of twilight and tree shadows. Then came Alex, half-limping, half-shuffling through the layer of snow. He looked like a zombie. Skye was next, mother-henning Alex, warning him when he veered too close to a tree trunk, encouraging him. Josh came last. He was cold through and through, but he knew Alex had to be way colder.

They came out of the trees and approached the road. "You're doing good," Skye said.

"We're halfway there."

A lie, Josh knew, but they were making progress. And they were all alive. So far. But what about the next day, and the next? What would Corey's twisted mind cook up for them or someone else? Josh didn't want to wait to find out. They had to do something. He remembered the twelfth suggestion on the "Dynamic Dozen" poster: Tell an adult. It was time to tell an adult—someone who would really listen.

An icy breeze cut into them as they trudged along the shoulder of the road. Mark's pace slowed, his steps grew more deliberate. His shoulders slumped and his head bent low. Because of the weather? Josh didn't think so. He'd seen this unstrung version of Mark not long before, right after he'd pulled the little kid from the path of the speeding van. A superhero, wounded.

Mark raised his eyes and gazed up at the sky, as if he'd just noticed the snow still swirling down. He pulled out his umbrella, popped it open, and angled it over his head, low.

A pickup neared, headlights on. Josh's mind was elsewhere—it was numb—so it was too late when he raised an arm and tried to flag down the truck. It rattled past. Then there was nothing but empty road and countryside and trees and dark and cold

"Where do you live, Alex?" Mark said.

Alex didn't answer. Maybe he was in a trance, maybe he'd turned into a Popsicle.

"WHERE DO YOU LIVE, ALEX?" Mark said.

"By school," Alex mumbled. "A block north of school."

"Good," Josh said.

"We're almost there," Skye said. They *were* closer. Josh decided they were going to make it.

"What will your parents say?" Josh said.

"What time is it?" Alex said.

Josh hit the light button on his watch. "A little after five."

"They won't be home," Alex said.

"Are you going to tell them?" Skye said.

Alex just slogged along.

"You have to tell them," she said.

"Let's just get him home," Josh said.

They turned off the road, passed the school, and at last got Alex to his house, a small, weathered place on a neat, grassy lot. A bent basketball hoop hung from the carport roof. Alex let himself in with his own key, luckily still in his frozen jeans. Skye followed him, then Mark and Josh. Alex turned up the heat and stood in the hallway, shivering, looking bewildered.

"The shower," Skye said. "You need to get out of those clothes and take a hot shower. Until you don't feel cold anymore."

Alex nodded. They followed him to his room, where he grabbed a dry change of clothes and shed Josh's coat. He went to the bathroom, and they heard the shower go on. Then they went to the kitchen to wait.

The house began to warm. The shower ran, on and on. Josh started to feel halfway comfortable. He hated the idea of going back outside, but he needed to get home. He wondered what Corey, Bunk, and Eli were doing right now. "Do they think they killed him?" he said.

"Do you think they're sorry?" Skye said. "Or at least worried?"

The shower went off.

"What next?" Josh said.

"THE SUPERHEROES LOOK FOR THEIR NEXT ADVENTURE," Mark said.

"Which will be putting an ending on this adventure," Skye said. "Who are we going to tell?"

"A grownup," Josh said. "Someone who will do something."

"Something," Mark said. His gaze was aimed right between Josh and Skye, aimed at . . . what? "Something," Mark repeated.

❄ 15 ❄
Threats

Skye and Mark were late the next morning. The temperature hung in the low teens, but Josh waited outside, pacing. When Skye finally showed, she was jogging, apple-cheeked. Alone.

"He didn't come," she said.

"Maybe later."

They hurried on, barely slowing at the intersection where Mark had performed his first superhero act.

"Where do you think he is?" Skye said.

"I don't know. Sick, maybe. Frozen, maybe."

"You think Alex will be at school?"

"I hope so," Josh said. "He'll be our star witness when we talk to Mrs. Drager." After

Corey and Bunk and Poor Rooney's Pond, the prospect of facing the principal seemed like no big deal.

Skye smiled. "We'll really ruffle Mrs. Benedict's feathers this time."

"Did you tell your dad?"

"Not yet," Skye said. "He got home late and he wasn't in a talking mood. Then he got upset because somebody kept phoning and hanging up. You tell your parents?"

Josh shook his head. He knew they'd find out soon, but he was putting it off. Telling them would mean admitting he'd lied about his plans for the afternoon. It would mean his mom—and dad, too—would have a hard time trusting him from now on. "I bet the hang-up calls were Corey," he said. "Checking to see if you were alive."

"You talked to him?"

"No, but someone kept calling us and hanging up, too. The caller ID said "Kitchens."

"I wonder if he knows Alex is alive."

"I'm sure Corey called him, too," Josh said. "Even if he cares zero about Alex, he'd care about himself."

"So maybe he knows."

"Maybe." But Josh hoped Corey didn't know. He hoped Corey hadn't slept a wink.

He hoped Corey's stomach felt like Josh's had out on that ice—filled with live worms and tied in a knot.

❋ ❋ ❋

Corey and Bunk were locked in a conversation at the school entrance. As soon as they saw Josh and Skye approaching, they hurried inside. In class, Alex avoided eye contact, but while Skye was up sharpening her pencil, she managed a short back-and-forth with him.

"He hasn't told anybody," she whispered to Josh as she slid into her chair.

"We need him to go with us," Josh said. "And Mark, too."

At lunch recess, Corey and Bunk shadowed Skye and Josh silently wherever they went.

Finally, Corey found his tongue. "We went by your classroom. Alex was there."

"No thanks to you," Skye said.

"You left him to die," Josh said.

Bunk looked as if he'd been slapped, but Corey stepped forward and pressed a finger against Josh's chest. "Don't say that again, Joshster."

"You left him to *die*," Josh repeated. He waited, flinching inside, for something to happen, but all he got from Corey was a you-made-the-wrong-choice-you-loser glare.

Josh knew *he* wasn't a loser. He knew he hadn't made the wrong choice. Finally.

"We were going for help," Bunk said.

"Couldn't find any?" Skye said.

Corey gave her a look. "That's our story, powder puff. We'll stick with it."

The bell rang. Josh and Skye started in. "We have to talk to Alex," Skye said.

"Afternoon recess," Josh said. "But if Mark and Alex won't go, we'll have to see Drager ourselves." There was no backing out now.

❄ ❄ ❄

Alex didn't want to come outside, but Josh and Skye convinced him they needed to talk. They headed for the soccer field. "Why haven't you told?" Josh said.

"Didn't you see Corey and Bunk come by our classroom?" Alex said. "They stood at the door and stared at me."

"They were afraid you were dead," Skye said.

"They weren't afraid," Alex said. "They want me dead."

"No they don't," Josh said. "You need to tell your parents."

"My dad wouldn't understand," Alex said, "how Corey could've made me go out on the ice. Why I wouldn't put up a fight."

"What about your mom?" Skye said.

"She'd freak out if she knew I almost drowned."

"She has to know," Josh said. "Somebody has to do something about Corey."

"We're going to Drager," Skye said. "Come with us."

"Our word against his," Alex said. "Him and his buddies."

"She has to believe us," Josh said. "Why would we lie?"

Alex looked up, then past Josh's shoulder. Josh turned, Skye turned. Corey and Bunk were twenty feet away, eyeing them. "I can't," Alex said.

Skye looked at Josh. She shrugged.

Suddenly Corey stood in front of them, daring them to move. Skye tried to go around them, but Bunk shoved her and sent her stumbling.

Corey turned to Josh. "You better tell your little girlfriend to keep her mouth shut, fat boy. You wouldn't want her to fall on her face and break those glasses, would you? You know what that would feel like—glass going in your eyes?"

"You wouldn't do that," Josh said, knowing he was probably wrong, that Corey's threat was probably serious. But suddenly he thought about Mark at the pond, and he had to fight back a smile. "You'd be in trouble until your beard turns gray."

"If she talks, I'm gonna do that," Corey said. "And I'm gonna get you, too." He looked from Josh to Alex and back again. "Both you fatties. And Sillycorn, too, if he ever has the guts to show up. I owe that little freak. You'll all wish you'd joined Poor Rooney at the bottom of his pond."

"You won't get anyone," Josh said, trying to sound sure of himself. "Come on, Skye, Alex."

Corey and Bunk stalked them until they neared the school entrance. "What are you gonna do, stay all night?" Corey called. "We'll be waiting."

"After school," Josh murmured to Skye. "After school we're going to Mrs. Drager whether Alex goes or not."

Back at the classroom, Skye nodded at Mark's empty chair. "Where is he?"

"Not coming." Maybe Mark was sick. A deep chill from the day before. Or maybe he was afraid. But Mark had never seemed afraid of much except stuff no one else was scared of: snowflakes; handshakes; too much weight on a bed; looking you in the eye.

"We're supposed to be watching out for him," Skye whispered. She removed her glasses and wiped the lenses on her sweater.

"How can we watch out for him if he's not here?" But Josh knew what Skye meant. Mark was tough but he was also fragile, as fragile as the glasses that Skye was perching back on her nose.

The afternoon dragged on. With about a half-hour to go, Ms. Murphy was distracted by something—or someone—outside the open classroom door. "Can I help you?" she said.

Josh heard a mumble. Across the room, Alex stared toward the door, then away, out the window. He swallowed, hard. Josh got a creepy, empty feeling in his chest. He knew it—Corey was out in the hall again, threatening Alex.

"Then you should be in your seventh-period class," she said to the person at the door. She watched for a moment before getting back to giving a homework assignment.

A few minutes later, Alex went to Ms. Murphy's desk. His coat was on, his backpack slung over his shoulder. He whispered to her and left, eyes on the floor. One star witness—*the* star witness—eliminated for now.

The end-of-day bell finally rang. Josh and Skye waited for the rest of the kids to empty from the classroom and halls, then made their way to the office. Josh trailed Skye through the open door and caught up with her at the counter, where she was peering down at the top of Mrs. Benedict's head. Mrs. Benedict looked up.

"What now?" she said. "I'm pretty sure I heard the bell ring, and the big clock on the wall says 3:35."

"We need to talk to Mrs. Drager," Skye said.

"Mrs. Drager is busy, busy, busy," Mrs. Benedict said.

"We need to see her," Josh said.

"She's in conference."

"She's always in conference," Josh said.

"Look," Mrs. Benedict said. "You're nice kids. I like you. I'm a nice guy. But I am the moat."

Josh looked at Mrs. Benedict's face. Stony. He looked at Mrs. Drager's door. Closed tight. Maybe she was in conference. "Come on, Skye."

"Where are you going?" she said as they arrived in the empty hallway.

"Nowhere," he said. "We'll wait here. She has to come out sometime." They stood just inside the main doors. It was warm, and they could see outside.

"What if she doesn't leave for a long time?"

"I don't have to be anywhere," Josh said. "Do you?"

Skye shook her head. "No."

Josh looked outside. "Corey and Bunk are out there."

"Look," Skye said, pointing.

Josh looked. Beyond Corey and Bunk, hurrying toward the school, was a kid wearing a yellow coat. "Mark."

He walked right up to Corey and Bunk, gesturing, holding up his blue lunch box.

"He's offering them food?" Skye said.

Corey grabbed for the lunch box and missed. Bunk tore off Mark's hat and threw it in the snow. Josh started for the door, Skye at his shoulder.

❋ 16 ❋
Evidence

I *want* to show them to you," Mark was saying to Corey as Josh and Skye arrived, skidding to a stop. "THEY'RE EVIDENCE."

"Evidence?" Corey said.

Mark took the lunchbox from behind his back, unzipped it, and pulled out a big plastic baggie filled with photos. He handed them to Corey. Everyone else crowded around to look.

The first one was a distance shot—from the side—of a group of kids heading down the shoulder of a road. Then a closer-up shot of the same kids: Corey, Bunk, Eli, Drew, Lee, Alex, Josh, Skye. On their way to Poor Rooney's.

The next picture showed the group at the pond. Eli was heading out, looking back, his face clearly visible.

"Four megapixels," Mark said.

In the next photo, Alex was sitting down with Drew and Lee, putting on his skates. The next one showed Corey grabbing him by the coat collar. Fear was plain on Alex's face, and still there in the next shot: Corey pulling him to his feet by the shoulders of his coat.

Bunk leaned closer as Corey uncovered the next one: Bunk pushing Skye to the ground. The action was captured perfectly—Skye halfway to the snow, glasses askew, Bunk with his arms extended. The next photo was similar, except it was Corey doing the pushing and Alex going for a tumble. The next picture showed Alex a few feet out on the ice, facing back toward Corey and Bunk, who stood elbow to elbow on the bank, making sure Alex didn't change his mind.

"Looks like there's quite a few more." Josh said. Something inside him smiled.

There *were* quite a few more. Bunk wrenching Skye away from Alex. Corey waving to Eli across the pond. Eli waving back into the zoom lens. Bunk throwing a rock at Alex. Corey throwing a rock. Bunk throwing another rock. A shot of Corey at the end of his throwing motion, and Alex, a rock bouncing off the ice at his feet.

"I'll kill you," Corey said to Mark. Mark didn't blink.

The next photo was an eye-catcher: Alex crashing through, water and shards of ice flying.

In the next one, Corey and Bunk were hurrying off the ice, past Skye and Josh, and Alex was in the distance, his head bobbing in the middle of a black patch of water. Then Skye was heading toward Alex. Corey and Bunk were taking off. Josh was tearing a big branch from the ground. Josh was racing back to the ice with the branch in tow. Skye and Josh were trying to pull Alex from the water. Alex was falling back in.

The shots got closer up as Corey peeled them off. Josh and Skye in the middle of a flurry of snowflakes, crouched near the hole, figuring out what to do next. Alex, wide-eyed, trying to hold on. Josh and Skye, heads turned toward the camera, surprise on their faces. Alex, a hint of hope on his. Close up, Josh and Skye mouthing words, Alex reaching out with one gloved hand.

Then, Josh remembered, Mark had stopped taking pictures. He'd been too busy helping. Still, one photo remained. Mark had printed it out big, on a full-size sheet of paper. In the picture Alex lay flat on his back by the hole, soaked, dripping, eyes closed. He looked dead. Josh and Skye knelt nearby. Mark, dressed in a suit and tie and his fishing hat, holding a Bible, stood over Alex. Surrounding them were Mark's mom and dad, another man and woman, a dozen or so kids from school, the van-dodging little kid and his two friends, Ms. Murphy holding a sign that said "Buddies, Not Bullies," Mrs. Benedict with her hand raised in a salute, a black-and-white bob-tailed sheep dog, and Abraham Lincoln. Off to one side was a policeman holding a bird cage. Behind its bars stood Corey and Bunk, miniaturized, looking scared. Off to the other side was a big gray hearse. The Grim Reaper sat behind the wheel.

They were all congregated on the thin ice in the middle of Poor Rooney's Pond. They'd come to Alex's funeral—Mark's version.

Corey stared at the picture. He held it closer to his face. "This one isn't real," he said, still staring.

"IT *COULD* BE REAL," Mark said. "ALEX HAD TO LOOK DEATH IN THE EYE."

"I didn't push him through the ice," Corey said.

"You made him go out there," Josh said. "He fell through because you forced him to go to the middle."

Corey shoved the pictures into his pocket. "You can have those," Mark said. "I have more in my backpack for Mrs. Drager. AND AN ENDLESS SUPPLY AT HOME."

"You're gonna show them to her?" Bunk said.

"Unless you go in with us and talk to her," Mark said. "Tell her the TRUTH."

Corey grabbed Mark's coat collar with one white-knuckled hand. "I ought to pound you," he said. "I should've made you all go out on the ice. Maybe you'd all be out of my life."

Josh and Skye each took one of Mark's arms and pulled him back a half-step. Corey let go. Mark picked up his hat.

"Mrs. Drager will be glad to know you're so sorry for what you did," Skye said.

Josh, Mark, and Skye started for the school. Josh felt the hair rise up on the back of his neck as he waited for something to slam into him from behind. A fist, a rock, something. When they were almost to the door, he glanced back. Corey and Bunk were following them, ten feet behind.

They arrived at the office. Skye peeked in. "Her door's still closed," she said. "The moat's still on alert."

They leaned against the wall in the hall-way, prepared to wait. Corey and Bunk joined them.

"No pictures if we talk to the Dragon?" Corey said.

"It depends on what you say," Mark said.

"If we tell the truth?" Corey said.

"Then no pictures," Mark said.

Josh heard the sound of a door opening. He leaned over and looked. A woman was coming out of the inner office. Mrs. Drager, he guessed. But she didn't look like a dragon. She was about Josh's mom's age with a round face and body and short spiky hair. Standing just outside her office, she said something to Mrs. Benedict, listened as Mrs. Benedict said something to her, then looked up and saw Josh.

"Josh Showalter?" she said, and Josh nodded. "Is Skye still with you?"

Skye moved over to the doorway.

"Just the people I wanted to see," Mrs. Drager said.

"Mark Silverthorn's here, too," Skye said.

"And Corey Kitchens," Josh said.

"And Bunk Bunker," Corey said, moving his head into Mrs. Drager's view, as if slipping it under the blade of a guillotine.

"Really?" Mrs. Drager said. "The whole cast of characters, huh?" She eyed them as they filed in. "Okay. In my office. Good guys and bad guys. You know who you are."

"We didn't mean to—" Corey began.

"Now," Mrs. Drager said, pointing at her half-opened door.

Skye went first, then Mark. By the time Josh walked into the small room, they were both staring back toward the outer wall, at a figure sitting in a chair.

"Hi," Alex said.

❄ **17** ❄
Cruising

Mrs. Drager sat down behind her desk, fingering a pen. She let her eyes move from person to person and come to rest on Corey. "If I were a police officer, I'd probably question each of you individually. And maybe that's what the police will do once they hear from me." Corey and Bunk looked at each other, grim-faced, surprised. "But right now I want all of you together.

"Alex was brave enough to come here," she said. "He just opened my door and said someone had tried to kill him. Then he told me a story that was scary and shocking. A story of scheming and lying and manipulating and bullying. And near-tragedy. And finally, intimidation so the story wouldn't come out.

"But it did come out, because Alex decided the intimidation wouldn't stop. He decided if Skye, Josh, and Mark could be courageous, he could, too. So I want to repeat what he told me, and let you fill in the blanks. Together we should be able to come up with a complete and final version of the crime." She eyed Corey, then Bunk, until they looked up at her. "Because that's what it was: a crime."

"A crime?" Corey whined. "But we're only thirteen. And they're making it sound worse—"

He stopped in mid-sentence. Mark had half-pulled a packet of pictures from his backpack.

"Worse than what?" Mrs. Drager said.

"Nothing," Bunk said as Corey stared at the floor.

Mrs. Drager began talking, referring to her notes from time to time. She asked questions and got responses, but Alex had told pretty much the whole story, even his part in encouraging Josh to go to the pond. There weren't many blanks to fill in, and Corey and Bunk had little to say until Mrs. Drager put down her pen and leaned back, studying them.

"We didn't think anything would happen," Corey whispered.

"You didn't think, period," Mrs. Drager said. "Once you came up with your awful plan to have someone go out on the ice to test it for you, you gave no thought to the consequences.

158

Or maybe you did, which is worse.

"When you ran away, you left Alex to die. If these three hadn't gone back, he would be dead. People would be talking about poor Alex instead of poor Rooney. And you two would be facing a murder charge."

Josh glanced at Corey and Bunk. Bunk was starting to cry. "This is only the beginning," Mrs. Drager told them. "In a few minutes I'm going to call the police, then your parents. We'll get them all in here and figure out the next step."

The office grew dead quiet. But not for long.

"THE DRAGON BREATHES FIRE," Mark said, sitting tall. "BAD GUYS WILT. GOOD GUYS WALK."

Mrs. Drager looked at Mark, a curious half-smile on her face. Then the half-smile spread. "You *are* good guys," she said. "*More* than good guys. You're heroes."

"SUPERHEROES?" Mark said.

"Almost," Mrs. Drager said. "The difference is that superheroes don't die. You *could* have died. All of you. You should have done what you could for Alex without going near him. One of you should have gone for help."

Josh knew she was right. They should have

159

stayed near shore and tried to throw Alex the branch or something to keep him up. But would he be dead now?

"I need to let your parents know what's going on," Mrs. Drager said. "So I'd like you four—Mark, Skye, Josh, and Alex—to wait in the outer office with Mrs. Benedict while I make some phone calls." She smiled, not drag-onlike at all. "Okay?"

"Okay," Josh said quickly. He still didn't consider himself a hero. He'd pretty much let Corey and Bunk push him around. He'd stood by while they bullied Skye and Mark. But at least he'd done the right thing at the end. Maybe next time he'd be brave faster. Maybe this would give him a start.

"One other thing," Mrs. Drager said as they stood. "I can live with being called 'the dragon.'" She smiled at Mark. "But this office is not the dragon's lair, and I'm sorry if you thought of it that way. Anytime any of you have a problem, my door will be open, and I'll be in here with a smile to greet you." She looked from face to face. "I'll make sure Mrs. Benedict knows that. Understood?"

They told her yes, then found seats in the outer office.

Josh felt exhausted suddenly. He wondered

what his mom and dad would say, whether they'd ever let him go to the pond again. But it didn't matter; he wanted to see them. In the chair next to him, Alex stretched out his legs and stared at his shoes.

"Sorry for trying to get you on the ice," he said to Josh.

"It's okay," Josh said. "They're pretty scary guys. I might have done the same thing."

"I doubt it," Alex said.

"You want the skates back?" Josh said. "I may not be needing them now."

"Nah," Alex said. "You earned 'em."

The police arrived. Mrs. Benedict directed the short man and tall woman into Mrs. Drager's office. Next came Corey's mother, then Bunk's parents, all looking as if they'd rather be anywhere else. Corey's father came in last, big and red-faced and full of bluster.

Twenty minutes later, Mrs. Drager's door opened. Silently, her office emptied. Bunk and his parents first, walking quickly, eyes straight ahead. Then Corey and his mom, followed by his dad, having a hushed heart-to-heart with the woman cop. The man cop stopped in Mrs. Drager's doorway, where he and Mrs. Drager talked for a moment. Josh thought maybe some-one—Corey or Bunk or their parents—would come over and tell Alex they were sorry. But they didn't give him a glance. In a moment they were gone, everyone but the cops.

They came and stood in front of Alex. The woman crouched down. "That was a brave thing you did, Alex, to tell Mrs. Drager," she said. "It's never easy to stand up to a bully. And it doesn't get any easier if you wait."

The man cop got down on a knee. "But you don't have to worry, now," he said. "Between us, the court system, the boys' parents, and Mrs. Drager, we don't expect any further trouble with those two or Eli Barnes or any of their friends, if they have any left."

"ALL THE PEOPLE LEFT," Mark said. "NO APOLOGIES TO ALEX. NO THANK-YOUS TO THE SUPERHEROES."

Officer Wells took a step back. The other cop—Blue, it said on her name tag—smiled at Mark. "They might be sorry," she said. "They might be thankful. But Mr. Kitchens talked to his lawyer before he got here. Lawyers don't like their clients to say they're sorry."

"But we're sorry it happened, Alex," Officer Wells said. "And we're thankful to your friends. We would've hated to pull you from the bottom of that pond. We would've hated telling your parents."

"But one thing would have been even worse," Officer Blue said. "Having to tell *all* your parents they had lost a child. It could have happened, too easily."

"So if there's a next time," said Officer Wells, "you need to use your heads, not just your brave hearts."

The officers left. More parents showed up. Alex's dad came first, then his mom. Josh had seen both of them before: they were two of the mourners at Alex's "funeral."

Mark's mom came in. "Still feeling better, Mark?" she said as she hurried toward Mrs. Drager's office.

Mark nodded. His face turned pink. He waited until she was out of hearing range. "I took more pictures this morning," he said, quietly for once. "Then I went home to work on all of them. I told my mom I felt sick."

Josh's mom came, then Skye's dad, who rushed up and lifted Skye out of her chair and hugged her close, her feet dangling. She squeezed him back, burying her face in his shoulder. "Sweetheart, thank God you're safe," he said, and Skye said something back, but her mouth was against her dad's coat, and Josh was trying not to listen.

Josh's dad arrived, looking worried but not

mad, and finally Mark's dad, wearing the FBI suit and tie. And a calm expression, as if he were used to stuff like this.

Finally Mrs. Drager's door opened again. The parents emerged, followed by Mrs. Drager. There were more hugs and lots of tears. Mark beamed.

They all went outside. Night had fallen. Josh breathed in the fresh, frosty air. It felt like heaven. Mark stared up at the black sky, the drifting flakes. He pulled up his hood. He angled both forearms over his head.

A charcoal-gray hearse—the hearse in Mark's picture—was parked among the cars in the lot. It was sparkly with a glaze of snow, and wide, and nearly twice as long as some of its neighbors. It was newer and fancier than the black one Josh's grandpa had ridden in two years earlier.

"You drove the coach, Dad?" Mark said accusingly. He dropped his arms.

Mark's dad looked a little embarrassed. "My car's being serviced, Mark. The coach was all I had on short notice."

"COOL," Alex said, walking around the hearse, inspecting it close up.

"Your dad works for a funeral home?" Skye asked Mark.

"I thought he was FBI," Josh said.

"My dad's the funeral director at Willow's Shade."

"You said he helps people," Josh said.

"He does," Mark said. "That's what he likes about his job."

"Mark's not so sure he likes it, though," Mark's mom said.

"I think it's great," Skye said.

"Me, too," Josh said, although he wasn't sure about the dead body part of it.

"You think so?" Mark said.

"COOL," Alex said again, patting a smooth front fender as if it were the shoulder of his faithful horse.

The parents stood in a cluster, admiring the hearse, too. "Free oil changes, Mr. Silverthorn," Alex's dad said. "As long as I'm manager of Rapid-Lube, you bring your vehicle in for whatever it needs, on the house."

"That's not necessary," Mark's dad said. "But thanks."

"Goes for the rest of you, too," Alex's dad said.

"Can we ride in it?" Alex said.

"Can we, Dad?" Mark said. "Can we give the kids a ride home?"

Mark's dad glanced at the other parents. He looked doubtful. "There aren't any seatbelts in back," he said.

"BECAUSE DEAD PEOPLE DON'T NEED SEATBELTS," Mark announced.

Skye's dad looked at Mark and chuckled. "It's okay with me," he said.

Josh's mom and dad eyed each other while Josh held his breath. They shrugged. "And us," his mom said.

Alex's mom and dad nodded.

Mark's dad opened up the back and they piled in. They sat on the thick carpet, facing each other across a row of silvery rollers built into the floor. Josh and Skye sat on one side, Alex and Mark on the other.

Mr. Silverthorn got in front and started the engine. The muffler rumbled softly beneath them. He put the hearse in gear, backed away, and eased out of the parking lot. It was quiet in the back, and nearly dark, and smelled of flowers. It was creepy in a good sort of way.

Mark's dad made a couple of turns, and then they were on the highway, rolling smoothly past the streets of Rathdrum.

"You're so lucky, Mark," Alex whispered, looking around, touching metal and fabric.

"You're lucky," Mark said, staring at the ceiling. "You could be making this journey in a casket."

"We all could," Alex said. "You guys could've ended up in the pond with me."

"THE FOUR SUPERHEROES CRUISE THROUGH THE NIGHT IN THEIR TOP-SECRET TRANSPORTER," Mark said. The headlights of an approaching car beamed into the back of the hearse, putting a glow on his pale skin. He was smiling, staring toward that in-between place again.

He turned his head, switching his gaze to Josh. He looked right into Josh's eyes, still smiling. Skye drew in a quick breath, almost silent. Josh felt an icy tingle melt into something warm.

The oncoming car whooshed past, returning the superheroes to the cover of darkness.

❄ About David Patneaude ❄

David Patneaude was born in St. Paul, Minnesota, but he has lived in the Seattle, Washington, area since he was six. He graduated from the University of Washington and served in the U.S. Navy.

He is also the author of *Someone Was Watching*, winner of the South Dakota Prairie Pasque Award and the Utah Children's Book Award; *The Last Man's Reward*, included on the New York Public Library's 1997 Books for the Teen Age; *Dark Starry Morning: Stories of This World and Beyond; Framed in Fire;* and *Haunting at Home Plate.* His books have been included on more than twenty state young readers' lists.

David lives in Woodinville, Washington, with his wife, Judy, and their two children, Jaime and Jeff. In his spare time he enjoys running, coaching, exploring the outdoors, and reading.